Dear Réné and Phuong,

I have asked permission to dedicate this book to you not only in memory of the happy evenings I have spent with you in Saigon over the last five years, but also because I have quite shamelessly borrowed the location of your flat to house one of my characters, and your name, Phuong, for the convenience of readers because it is simple, beautiful and easy to pronounce, which is not true of all your country-women's names. You will both realize I have borrowed little else, certainly not the characters of anyone in Viet Nam. Pyle, Granger, Fowler, Vigot, Joe – these have had no originals in the life of Saigon or Hanoi, and General Thé is dead: shot in the back, so they say. Even the historical events have been in at least one case rearranged. For example, the big bomb near the Continental preceded and did not follow the bicycle bombs. I have no scruples about such small changes. This is a story and not a piece of history, and I hope that as a story about a few imaginary characters it will pass for both of you one hot Saigon evening.

Yours affectionately,

Graham Greene

GRAHAM GREENE

THE QUIET AMERICAN

82

n on or before the last date

PENGUIN BOOKS
in association with William Heinemann Ltd

PENGUIN BOOKS

Published by the Penguin Group
Penguin Books Ltd, 27 Wrights Lane, London W8 5TZ, England
Penguin Putnam Inc., 375 Hudson Street, New York, New York 10014, USA
Penguin Books Australia Ltd, Ringwood, Victoria, Australia
Penguin Books Canada Ltd, 10 Alcorn Avenue, Toronto, Ontario, Canada M4V 3B2
Penguin Books (NZ) Ltd, Private Bag 102902, NSMC, Auckland, New Zealand

Penguin Books Ltd, Registered Offices: Harmondsworth, Middlesex, England

First published in Great Britain by William Heinemann Ltd 1955
First published in the United States of America by Viking Press 1956
Viking Compass Edition published 1957
Published in Penguin Books in Great Britain 1962
Reset and reprinted in Penguin Books from the Collected Edition
in Great Britain 1974 and in the USA 1977

Copyright © Graham Greene, 1973
All rights reserved

Printed in England by Clays Ltd, St Ives plc
Set in Linotype Times

THE QUIET AMERICAN

Graham Greene was born in 1904. On coming down from Balliol College, Oxford, he worked for four years as sub-editor on *The Times*. He established his reputation with his fourth novel, *Stamboul Train*. In 1935 he made a journey across Liberia, described in *Journey Without Maps*, and on his return was appointed film critic of the *Spectator*. In 1926 he had been received into the Roman Catholic Church and visited Mexico in 1938 to report on the religious persecution there. As a result he wrote *The Lawless Roads* and, later, his famous novel *The Power and the Glory*. *Brighton Rock* was published in 1938 and in 1940 he became literary editor of the *Spectator*. The next year he undertook work for the Foreign Office and was stationed in Sierra Leone from 1941 to 1943. This later produced his novel, *The Heart of the Matter*, set in West Africa.

As well as his many novels, Graham Greene wrote several collections of short stories, four travel books, six plays, three books of auto-biography – *A Sort of Life*, *Ways of Escape* and *A World of My Own* (published posthumously) – two of biography and four books for children. He also contributed hundreds of essays, and film and book reviews, some of which appear in *Reflections*. Many of his novels and short stories have been filmed and *The Third Man* was written as a film treatment. A great number of his film writings, reviews, scripts and interviews have been published as *Mornings in the Dark: A Graham Greene Film Reader* (1993). Graham Greene was a member of the Order of Merit and a Companion of Honour.

Graham Greene died in April 1991. Among the many people who paid tribute to him on his death were Kingsley Amis: 'He will be missed all over the world. Until today, he was our greatest living novelist'; Alec Guinness: 'He was a great writer who spoke brilliantly to a whole generation. He was almost prophet-like with a surprising humility'; and William Golding: 'Graham Greene was in a class by himself ... He will be read and remembered as the ultimate chronicler of twentieth-century man's consciousness and anxiety'.

'I do not like being moved: for the will is
   excited; and action
Is a most dangerous thing; I tremble for
   something factitious,
Some malpractice of heart and illegitimate
   process;
We're so prone to these things, with our
   terrible notions of duty.'
                              A. H. CLOUGH

'This is the patent age of new inventions
   For killing bodies, and for saving souls,
All propagated with the best intentions.'
                              BYRON

PART ONE

Chapter 1

AFTER dinner I sat and waited for Pyle in my room over the rue Catinat; he had said, 'I'll be with you at latest by ten,' and when midnight struck I couldn't stay quiet any longer and went down into the street. A lot of old women in black trousers squatted on the landing: it was February and I suppose too hot for them in bed. One trishaw driver pedalled slowly by towards the river-front and I could see lamps burning where they had disembarked the new American planes. There was no sign of Pyle anywhere in the long street.

Of course, I told myself, he might have been detained for some reason at the American Legation, but surely in that case he would have telephoned to the restaurant – he was very meticulous about small courtesies. I turned to go indoors when I saw a girl waiting in the next doorway. I couldn't see her face, only the white silk trousers and the long flowered robe, but I knew her for all that. She had so often waited for me to come home at just this place and hour.

'Phuong,' I said – which means Phoenix, but nothing nowadays is fabulous and nothing rises from its ashes. I knew before she had time to tell me that she was waiting for Pyle too. 'He isn't here.'

'*Je sais. Je t'ai vu seul à la fenêtre.*'

'You may as well wait upstairs,' I said. 'He will be coming soon.'

'I can wait here.'

'Better not. The police might pick you up.'

She followed me upstairs. I thought of several ironic and unpleasant jests I might make, but neither her English nor her French would have been good enough for her to understand the irony, and, strange to say, I had no desire to hurt her or even to hurt myself. When we reached the landing all the old women turned their heads, and as soon as we had passed their voices rose and fell as though they were singing together.

'What are they talking about?'

11

'They think I have come home.'

Inside my room the tree I had set up weeks ago for the Chinese New Year had shed most of its yellow blossoms. They had fallen between the keys of my typewriter. I picked them out. '*Tu es troublé*,' Phuong said.

'It's unlike him. He's such a punctual man.'

I took off my tie and my shoes and lay down on the bed. Phuong lit the gas stove and began to boil the water for tea. It might have been six months ago. 'He says you are going away soon now,' she said.

'Perhaps.'

'He is very fond of you.'

'Thank him for nothing,' I said.

I saw that she was doing her hair differently, allowing it to fall black and straight over her shoulders. I remembered that Pyle had once criticized the elaborate hairdressing which she thought became the daughter of a mandarin. I shut my eyes and she was again the same as she used to be: she was the hiss of steam, the clink of a cup, she was a certain hour of the night and the promise of rest.

'He will not be long,' she said as though I needed comfort for his absence.

I wondered what they talked about together. Pyle was very earnest and I had suffered from his lectures on the Far East, which he had known for as many months as I had years. Democracy was another subject of his – he had pronounced and aggravating views on what the United States was doing for the world. Phuong on the other hand was wonderfully ignorant; if Hitler had come into the conversation she would have interrupted to ask who he was. The explanation would be all the more difficult because she had never met a German or a Pole and had only the vaguest knowledge of European geography, though about Princess Margaret of course she knew more than I. I heard her put a tray down on the end of the bed.

'Is he still in love with you, Phuong?'

To take an Annamite to bed with you is like taking a bird: they twitter and sing on your pillow. There had been a time when I thought none of their voices sang like Phuong's. I put out my hand and touched her arm – their bones too were as fragile as a bird's.

'Is he, Phuong?'

She laughed and I heard her strike a match. 'In love?' – perhaps it was one of the phrases she didn't understand.

'May I make your pipe?' she asked.

When I opened my eyes she had lit the lamp and the tray was already prepared. The lamplight made her skin the colour of dark amber as she bent over the flame with a frown of concentration, heating the small paste of opium, twirling her needle.

'Does Pyle still not smoke?' I asked her.

'No.'

'You ought to make him or he won't come back.' It was a superstition among them that a lover who smoked would always return, even from France. A man's sexual capacity might be injured by smoking, but they would always prefer a faithful to a potent lover. Now she was kneading the little ball of hot paste on the convex margin of the bowl and I could smell the opium. There is no smell like it. Beside the bed my alarm-clock showed twelve-twenty, but already my tension was over. Pyle had diminished. The lamp lit her face as she tended the long pipe, bent over it with the serious attention she might have given to a child. I was fond of my pipe: more than two feet of straight bamboo, ivory at either end. Two-thirds of the way down was the bowl, like a convolvulus reversed, the convex margin polished and darkened by the frequent kneading of the opium. Now with a flick of the wrist she plunged the needle into the tiny cavity, released the opium and reversed the bowl over the flame, holding the pipe steady for me. The bead of opium bubbled gently and smoothly as I inhaled.

The practised inhaler can draw a whole pipe down in one breath, but I always had to take several pulls. Then I lay back, with my neck on the leather pillow, while she prepared the second pipe.

I said, 'You know, really, it's as clear as daylight. Pyle knows I smoke a few pipes before bed, and he doesn't want to disturb me. He'll be round in the morning.'

13

In went the needle and I took my second pipe. As I laid it down, I said, 'Nothing to worry about. Nothing to worry about at all.' I took a sip of tea and held my hand in the pit of her arm. 'When you left me,' I said, 'it was lucky I had this to fall back on. There's a good house in the rue d'Ormay. What a fuss we Europeans make about nothing. You shouldn't live with a man who doesn't smoke, Phuong.'

'But he's going to marry me,' she said. 'Soon now.'

'Of course, that's another matter.'

'Shall I make your pipe again?'

'Yes.'

I wondered whether she would consent to sleep with me that night if Pyle never came, but I knew that when I had smoked four pipes I would no longer want her. Of course it would be agreeable to feel her thigh beside me in the bed – she always slept on her back, and when I woke in the morning I could start the day with a pipe, instead of with my own company. 'Pyle won't come now,' I said. 'Stay here, Phuong.' She held the pipe out to me and shook her head. By the time I had drawn the opium in, her presence or absence mattered very little.

'Why is Pyle not here?' she asked.

'How do I know?' I said.

'Did he go to see General Thé?'

'I wouldn't know.'

'He told me if he could not have dinner with you, he wouldn't come here.'

'Don't worry. He'll come. Make me another pipe.' When she bent over the flame the poem of Baudelaire's came into my mind: '*Mon enfant, ma soeur ...*' How did it go on?

> *Aimer à loisir,*
> *Aimer et mourir*
> *Au pays qui te ressemble.*

Out on the waterfront slept the ships, '*dont l'humeur est vagabonde*'. I thought that if I smelt her skin it would have the faintest fragrance of opium, and her colour was that of the small flame. I had seen the flowers on her dress beside the canals in the north, she was indigenous like a herb, and I never wanted to go home.

'I wish I were Pyle,' I said aloud, but the pain was limited and bearable – the opium saw to that. Somebody knocked on the door.

'Pyle,' she said.

'No. It's not his knock.'

Somebody knocked again impatiently. She got quickly up, shaking the yellow tree so that it showered its petals again over my typewriter. The door opened. 'Monsieur Fowlair,' a voice commanded.

'I'm Fowler,' I said. I was not going to get up for a policeman – I could see his khaki shorts without lifting my head.

He explained in almost unintelligible Vietnamese French that I was needed immediately – at once – rapidly – at the Sureté.

'At the French Sureté or the Vietnamese?'

'The French.' In his mouth the word sounded like *'Françung'*.

'What about?'

He didn't know: it was his orders to fetch me.

'Toi aussi,' he said to Phuong.

'Say *vous* when you speak to a lady,' I told him. 'How did you know she was here?'

He only repeated that they were his orders.

'I'll come in the morning.'

'Sur le chung,' he said, a little, neat, obstinate figure. There wasn't any point in arguing, so I got up and put on my tie and shoes. Here the police had the last word: they could withdraw my order of circulation: they could have me barred from Press Conferences: they could even, if they chose, refuse me an exit permit. These were the open legal methods, but legality was not essential in a country at war. I knew a man who had suddenly and inexplicably lost his cook – he had traced him to the Vietnamese Sureté, but the officers there assured him that he had been released after questioning. His family never saw him again. Perhaps he had joined the Communists; perhaps he had been enlisted in one of the private armies which flourished round Saigon – the Hoa-Haos or the Caodaists or General Thé. Perhaps he was in a French prison. Perhaps he was happily making money out of girls in Cholon,

15

the Chinese suburb. Perhaps his heart had given way when they questioned him. I said, 'I'm not going to walk. You'll have to pay for a trishaw.' One had to keep one's dignity.

That was why I refused a cigarette from the French officer at the Sureté. After three pipes I felt my mind clear and alert: it could take such decisions easily without losing sight of the main question – what do they want from me? I had met Vigot before several times at parties – I had noticed him because he appeared incongruously in love with his wife, who ignored him, a flashy and false blonde. Now it was two in the morning and he sat tired and depressed in the cigarette smoke and the heavy heat, wearing a green eye-shade, and he had a volume of Pascal open on his desk to while away the time. When I refused to allow him to question Phuong without me he gave way at once, with a single sigh that might have represented his weariness with Saigon, with the heat, or with the whole human condition.

He said in English, 'I'm so sorry I had to ask you to come.'

'I wasn't asked. I was ordered.'

'Oh, these native police – they don't understand.' His eyes were on a page of *Les Pensées* as though he were still absorbed in those sad arguments. 'I wanted to ask you a few questions – about Pyle.'

'You had better ask him the questions.'

He turned to Phuong and interrogated her sharply in French. 'How long have you lived with Monsieur Pyle?'

'A month – I don't know,' she said.

'How much has he paid you?'

'You've no right to ask her that,' I said. 'She's not for sale.'

'She used to live with you, didn't she?' he asked abruptly.

'For two years.'

'I'm a correspondent who's supposed to report your war – when you let him. Don't ask me to contribute to your scandal sheet as well.'

'What do you know about Pyle? Please answer my questions, Monsieur Fowler. I don't want to ask them. But this is serious. Please believe me it is very serious.'

'I'm not an informer. You know all I can tell you about

16

Pyle. Age thirty-two, employed in the Economic Aid Mission, nationality American.'

'You sound like a friend of his,' Vigot said, looking past me at Phuong. A native policeman came in with three cups of black coffee.

'Or would you rather have tea?' Vigot asked.

'I *am* a friend,' I said. 'Why not? I shall be going home one day, won't I? I can't take her with me. She'll be all right with him. It's a reasonable arrangement. And he's going to marry her, he says. He might, you know. He's a good chap in his way. Serious. Not one of those noisy bastards at the Continental. A quiet American,' I summed him precisely up as I might have said, 'a blue lizard', 'a white elephant'.

Vigot said, 'Yes.' He seemed to be looking for words on his desk with which to convey his meaning as precisely as I had done. 'A very quiet American.' He sat there in the little hot office waiting for one of us to speak. A mosquito droned to the attack and I watched Phuong. Opium makes you quick-witted – perhaps only because it calms the nerves and stills the emotions. Nothing, not even death, seems so important. Phuong, I thought, had not caught his tone, melancholy and final, and her English was very bad. While she sat there on the hard office-chair, she was still waiting patiently for Pyle. I had at that moment given up waiting, and I could see Vigot taking those two facts in.

'How did you meet him first?' Vigot asked me.

Why should I explain to him that it was Pyle who had met me? I had seen him last September coming across the square towards the bar of the Continental: an unmistakably young and unused face flung at us like a dart. With his gangly legs and his crew-cut and his wide campus gaze he seemed incapable of harm. The tables on the street were most of them full. 'Do you mind?' he had asked with serious courtesy. 'My name's Pyle. I'm new here,' and he had folded himself around a chair and ordered a beer. Then he looked quickly up into the hard noon glare.

'Was that a grenade?' he asked with excitement and hope.

'Most likely the exhaust of a car,' I said, and was suddenly

17

sorry for his disappointment. One forgets so quickly one's own youth: once I was interested myself in what for want of a better term they call news. But grenades had staled on me; they were something listed on the back page of the local paper – so many last night in Saigon, so many in Cholon: they never made the European Press. Up the street came the lovely flat figures – the white silk trousers, the long tight jackets in pink and mauve patterns slit up the thigh. I watched them with the nostalgia I knew I would feel when I had left these regions for ever. 'They are lovely, aren't they?' I said over my beer, and Pyle cast them a cursory glance as they went up the rue Catinat.

'Oh, sure,' he said indifferently: he was a serious type. 'The Minister's very concerned about these grenades. It would be very awkward, he says, if there was an incident – with one of us, I mean.'

'With one of you? Yes, I suppose that would be serious. Congress wouldn't like it.' Why does one want to tease the innocent? Perhaps only ten days ago he had been walking back across the Common in Boston, his arms full of the books he had been reading in advance on the Far East and the problems of China. He didn't even hear what I said; he was absorbed already in the dilemmas of Democracy and the responsibilities of the West; he was determined – I learnt that very soon – to do good, not to any individual person but to a country, a continent, a world. Well, he was in his element now with the whole universe to improve.

'Is he in the mortuary?' I asked Vigot.

'How did you know he was dead?' It was a foolish policeman's question, unworthy of the man who read Pascal, unworthy also of the man who so strangely loved his wife. You cannot love without intuition.

'Not guilty,' I said. I told myself that it was true. Didn't Pyle always go his own way? I looked for any feeling in myself, even resentment at a policeman's suspicion, but I could find none. No one but Pyle was responsible. Aren't we all better dead? the opium reasoned within me. But I looked cautiously at Phuong, for it was hard on her. She must have loved him in her way: hadn't she been fond of me and hadn't

18

she left me for Pyle? She had attached herself to youth and hope and seriousness and now they had failed her more than age and despair. She sat there looking at the two of us and I thought she had not yet understood. Perhaps it would be a good thing if I could get her away before the fact got home. I was ready to answer any questions if I could bring the interview quickly and ambiguously to an end, so that I might tell her later, in private, away from a policeman's eye and the hard office chairs and the bare globe where the moths circled.

I said to Vigot, 'What hours are you interested in?'

'Between six and ten.'

'I had a drink at the Continental at six. The waiters will remember. At six forty-five I walked down to the quay to watch the American planes unloaded. I saw Wilkins of the Associated News by the door of the Majestic. Then I went into the cinema next door. They'll probably remember – they had to get me change. From there I took a trishaw to the Vieux Moulin – I suppose I arrived about eight thirty – and had dinner by myself. Granger was there – you can ask him. Then I took a trishaw back about a quarter to ten. You could probably find the driver. I was expecting Pyle at ten, but he didn't turn up.'

'Why were you expecting him?'

'He telephoned me. He said he had to see me about something important.'

'Have you any idea what?'

'No. Everything was important to Pyle.'

'And this girl of his? – do you know where she was?'

'She was waiting for him outside at midnight. She was anxious. She knows nothing. Why, can't you see she's waiting for him still?'

'Yes,' he said.

'And you can't really believe I killed him for jealousy – or she for what? He was going to marry her.'

'Yes.'

'Where did you find him?'

'He was in the water under the bridge to Dakow.'

The Vieux Moulin stood beside the bridge. There were armed police on the bridge and the restaurant had an iron grille to keep out grenades. It wasn't safe to cross the bridge at night, for all the far side of the river was in the hands of the Vietminh after dark. I must have dined within fifty yards of his body.

'The trouble was,' I said, 'he got mixed up.'

'To speak plainly,' Vigot said, 'I am not altogether sorry. He was doing a lot of harm.'

'God save us always,' I said, 'from the innocent and the good.'

'The good?'

'Yes, good. In his way. You're a Roman Catholic. You wouldn't recognize his way. And anyway, he was a damned Yankee.'

'Would you mind identifying him? I'm sorry. It's a routine, not a very nice routine.'

I didn't bother to ask him why he didn't wait for someone from the American Legation, for I knew the reason. French methods are a little old-fashioned by our cold standards: they believe in the conscience, the sense of guilt, a criminal should be confronted with his crime, for he may break down and betray himself. I told myself again I was innocent, while he went down the stone stairs to where the refrigerating plant hummed in the basement.

They pulled him out like a tray of ice-cubes, and I looked at him. The wounds were frozen into placidity. I said, 'You see, they don't re-open in my presence.'

'*Comment*?'

'Isn't that one of the objects? Ordeal by something or other? But you've frozen him stiff. They didn't have deep freezes in the Middle Ages.'

'You recognize him?'

'Oh yes.'

He looked more than ever out of place: he should have stayed at home. I saw him in a family snapshot album, riding on a dude ranch, bathing on Long Island, photographed with his colleagues in some apartment on the twenty-third floor. He belonged to the skyscraper and the express elevator, the ice-cream and the dry Martinis, milk at lunch, and chicken sandwiches on the Merchant Limited.

'He wasn't dead from this,' Vigot said, pointing at a wound in the chest. 'He was drowned in the mud. We found the mud in his lungs.'

'You work quickly.'

'One has to in this climate.'

They pushed the tray back and closed the door. The rubber padded.

'You can't help us at all?' Vigot asked.

'Not at all.'

I walked back with Phuong towards my flat. I was no longer on my dignity. Death takes away vanity – even the vanity of the cuckold who mustn't show his pain. She was still unaware of what it was about, and I had no technique for telling her slowly and gently. I was a correspondent: I thought in headlines. 'American official murdered in Saigon.' Working on a newspaper one does not learn the way to break bad news, and even now I had to think of my paper and to ask her, 'Do you mind stopping at the cable office?' I left her in the street and sent my wire and came back to her. It was only a gesture: I knew too well that the French correspondents would already be informed, or if Vigot had played fair (which was possible), then the censors would hold my telegram till the French had filed theirs. My paper would get the news first under a Paris date-line. Not that Pyle was very important. It wouldn't have done to cable the details of his true career, that before he died he had been responsible for at least fifty deaths, for it would have damaged Anglo-American relations, the Minister would have been upset. The Minister had a great respect for Pyle – Pyle had taken a good degree in – well, one of those subjects Americans can take degrees in: perhaps public relations or theatrecraft, perhaps even Far Eastern studies (he had read a lot of books).

'Where is Pyle?' Phuong asked. 'What did they want?'

'Come home,' I said.

'Will Pyle come?'

'He's as likely to come there as anywhere else.'

The old women were still gossiping on the landing, in the relative cool. When I opened my door I could tell my room had been searched: everything was tidier than I ever left it.

'Another pipe?' Phuong asked.

'Yes.'

I took off my tie and my shoes; the interlude was over; the night was nearly the same as it had been. Phuong crouched at the end of the bed and lit the lamp. *Mon enfant, ma soeur* – skin the colour of amber. *Sa douce langue natale.*

'Phuong,' I said. She was kneading the opium on the bowl. '*Il est mort,* Phuong.' She held the needle in her hand and looked up at me like a child trying to concentrate, frowning. '*Tu dis?*'

'Pyle *est mort. Assassiné.*'

She put the needle down and sat back on her heels, looking at me. There was no scene, no tears, just thought – the long private thought of somebody who has to alter a whole course of life.

'You had better stay here tonight,' I said.

She nodded and taking up the needle again began to heat the opium. That night I woke from one of those short deep opium sleeps, ten minutes long, that seem a whole night's rest, and found my hand where it had always lain at night, between her legs. She was asleep and I could hardly hear her breathing. Once again after so many months I was not alone, and yet I thought suddenly with anger, remembering Vigot and his eye-shade in the police station and the quiet corridors of the Legation with no one about and the soft hairless skin under my hand, 'Am I the only one who really cared for Pyle?'

Chapter 2

1

THE morning Pyle arrived in the square by the Continental I had seen enough of my American colleagues of the Press, big, noisy, boyish and middle-aged, full of sour cracks against the French, who were, when all was said, fighting this war. Periodically, after an engagement had been tidily finished and the casualties removed from the scene, they would be summoned to Hanoi, nearly four hours' flight away, addressed by the Commander-in-Chief, lodged for one night in a Press Camp where they boasted that the barman was the best in Indo-China, flown over the late battlefield at a height of 3,000 feet (the limit of a heavy machine-gun's range) and then delivered safely and noisily back, like a school-treat, to the Continental Hotel in Saigon.

Pyle was quiet, he seemed modest, sometimes that first day I had to lean forward to catch what he was saying. And he was very, very serious. Several times he seemed to shrink up within himself at the noise of the American Press on the terrace above – the terrace which was popularly believed to be safer from hand-grenades. But he criticized nobody.

'Have you read York Harding?' he asked.

'No. No, I don't think so. What did he write?'

He gazed at a milk-bar across the street and said dreamily, 'That looks like a soda-fountain.' I wondered what depth of homesickness lay behind his odd choice of what to observe in a scene so unfamiliar. But hadn't I on my first walk up the rue Catinat noticed first the shop with the Guerlain perfume and comforted myself with the thought that, after all, Europe was only distant thirty hours? He looked reluctantly away from the milk-bar and said, 'York wrote a book called *The Advance of Red China*. It's a very profound book.'

'I haven't read it. Do you know him?'

He nodded solemnly and lapsed into silence. But he broke it again a moment later to modify the impression he had given. 'I don't know him well,' he said. 'I guess I only met him twice.' I liked him for that – to consider it was boasting to claim acquaintance with – what was his name? – York Harding. I was to learn later that he had an enormous respect for what he called serious writers. That term excluded novelists, poets and dramatists unless they had what he called a contemporary theme, and even then it was better to read the straight stuff as you got it from York.

I said, 'You know, if you live in a place for long you cease to read about it.'

'Of course I always like to know what the man on the spot has to say,' he replied guardedly.

'And then check it with York?'

'Yes.' Perhaps he had noticed the irony, because he added with his habitual politeness, 'I'd take it as a very great privilege if you could find time to brief me on the main points. You see, York was here more than two years ago.'

I liked his loyalty to Harding – whoever Harding was. It was a change from the denigrations of the Pressmen and their immature cynicism. I said, 'Have another bottle of beer and I'll try to give you an idea of things.'

I began, while he watched me intently like a prize pupil, by explaining the situation in the north, in Tonkin, where the French in those days were hanging on to the delta of the Red River, which contained Hanoi and the only northern port, Haiphong. Here most of the rice was grown, and when the harvest was ready the annual battle for the rice always began.

'That's the north,' I said. 'The French may hold, poor devils, if the Chinese don't come to help the Vietminh. A war of jungle and mountain and marsh, paddy fields where you wade shoulder-high and the enemy simply disappear, bury their arms, put on peasant dress. But you can rot comfortably in the damp in Hanoi. They don't throw bombs there. God knows why. You could call it a regular war.'

'And here in the south?'

'The French control the main roads until seven in the evening: they control the watch towers after that, and the towns – part of them. That doesn't mean you are safe, or there wouldn't be iron grilles in front of the restaurants.'

How often I had explained all this before. I was a record always turned on for the benefit of newcomers – the visiting Member of Parliament, the new British Minister. Sometimes I would wake up in the night saying, 'Take the case of the Caodaists.' Or the Hoa-Haos or the Binh Xuyen, all the private armies who sold their services for money or revenge. Strangers found them picturesque, but there is nothing picturesque in treachery and distrust.

'And now,' I said, 'there's General Thé. He was Caodaist Chief of Staff, but he's taken to the hills to fight both sides, the French, the Communists . . .'

'York,' Pyle said, 'wrote that what the East needed was a Third Force.' Perhaps I should have seen that fanatic gleam, the quick response to a phrase, the magic sound of figures: Fifth Column, Third Force, Seventh Day. I might have saved all of us a lot of trouble, even Pyle, if I had realized the direction of that indefatigable young brain. But I left him with arid bones of background and took my daily walk up and down the rue Catinat. He would have to learn for himself the real background that held you as a smell does: the gold of the rice-fields under a flat late sun: the fishers' fragile cranes hovering over the fields like mosquitoes: the cups of tea on an old abbot's platform, with his bed and his commercial calendars, his buckets and broken cups and the junk of a life-time washed up around his chair: the mollusc hats of the girls repairing the road where a mine had burst: the gold and the young green and the bright dresses of the south, and in the north the deep browns and the black clothes and the circle of enemy mountains and the drone of planes. When I first came I counted the days of my assignment, like a schoolboy marking off the days of term; I thought I was tied to what was left of a Bloomsbury square and the 73 bus passing the portico of Euston and springtime in the local in Torrington Place. Now the bulbs would be out in the square garden, and I didn't care a damn. I wanted a day punctuated by those quick reports that might be car-exhausts or might be grenades, I wanted to keep the sight of those silk-trousered figures moving with grace through the humid noon, I wanted Phuong, and my home had shifted its ground eight thousand miles.

I turned at the High Commissioner's house, where the Foreign Legion stood on guard in their white képis and their scarlet epaulettes, crossed by the Cathedral and came back by the dreary wall of the Vietnamese Sureté that seemed to smell of urine and injustice. And yet that too was a part of home, like the dark passages on upper floors one avoided in childhood. The new dirty magazines were out on the bookstalls near the quay – *Tabu* and *Illusion*, and the sailors were drinking beer on the pavement, an easy mark for a home-made bomb. I thought of Phuong, who would be haggling over the price of fish in the third street down on the left before going for her elevenses to the milk-bar (I always knew where she was in those days), and Pyle ran easily and naturally out of my mind. I didn't even mention him to Phuong, when we sat down to lunch together in our room over the rue Catinat and she wore her best flowered silk robe because it was two years to a day since we had met in the Grand Monde in Cholon.

2

Neither of us mentioned him when we woke on the morning after his death. Phuong had risen before I was properly awake and had our tea ready. One is not jealous of the dead, and it seemed easy to me that morning to take up our old life together.

'Will you stay tonight?' I asked Phuong over the *croissants* as casually as I could.

'I will have to fetch my box.'

'The police may be there,' I said. 'I had better come with you.' It was the nearest we came that day to speaking of Pyle.

Pyle had a flat in a new villa near the rue Duranton, off one of those main streets which the French continually subdivided in honour of their generals – so that the rue de Gaulle became after the third intersection the rue Leclerc, and that again sooner or later would probably turn abruptly into the rue de Lattre. Somebody important must have been arriving from Europe by air, for there was a policeman facing the pavement every twenty yards along the route to the High Commissioner's Residence.

On the gravel drive to Pyle's apartment were several motor-cycles and a Vietnamese policeman examined my press-card. He wouldn't allow Phuong into the house, so I went in search of a French officer. In Pyle's bathroom Vigot was washing his hands with Pyle's soap and drying them on Pyle's towel. His tropical suit had a stain of oil on the sleeve – Pyle's oil, I supposed.

'Any news?' I asked.

'We found his car in the garage. It's empty of petrol. He must have gone off last night in a trishaw – or in somebody else's car. Perhaps the petrol was drained away.'

'He might even have walked,' I said. 'You know what Americans are.'

'Your car was burnt, wasn't it?' he went thoughtfully on. 'You haven't a new one yet?'

'No.'

'It's not an important point.'

'No.'

'Have you any views?' he asked.

'Too many,' I said.

'Tell me.'

'Well, he might have been murdered by the Vietminh. They have murdered plenty of people in Saigon. His body was found in the river by the bridge to Dakow – Vietminh territory when your police withdraw at night. Or he might have been killed by the Vietnamese Sureté – it's been known. Perhaps they didn't like his friends. Perhaps he was killed by Caodaists because he knew General Thé.'

'Did he?'

'They say so. Perhaps he was killed by General Thé because he knew the Caodaists. Perhaps he was killed by the Hoa-Haos for making passes at the General's concubines. Perhaps he was just killed by someone who wanted his money.'

'Or a simple case of jealousy,' Vigot said.

'Or perhaps by the French Sureté,' I continued, 'because they didn't like his contacts. Are you really looking for the people who killed him?'

'No,' Vigot said. 'I'm just making a report, that's all. So long as it's an act of war – well, there are thousands killed every year.'

'You can rule me out,' I said. 'I'm not involved. Not involved,' I repeated. It had been an article of my creed. The human condition being what it was, let them fight, let them love, let them murder, I would not be involved. My fellow journalists called themselves correspondents; I preferred the title of reporter. I wrote what I saw. I took no action – even an opinion is a kind of action.

'What are you doing here?'

'I've come for Phuong's belongings. Your police wouldn't let her in.'

'Well, let us go and find them.'

'It's nice of you, Vigot.'

Pyle had two rooms, a kitchen and bathroom. We went to the bedroom. I knew where Phuong would keep her box – under the bed. We pulled it out together; it contained her picture books. I took her few spare clothes out of the wardrobe, her two good robes and her spare trousers. One had a sense that they had been hanging there for a few hours only and didn't belong, they were in passage like a butterfly in a room. In a drawer I found her small triangular *culottes* and her collection of scarves. There was really very little to put in the box, less than a week-end visitor's at home.

In the sitting-room there was a photograph of herself and Pyle. They had been photographed in the botanical gardens beside a large stone dragon. She held Pyle's dog on a leash – a black chow with a black tongue. A too black dog. I put the photograph in her box. 'What's happened to the dog?' I said.

'It isn't here. He may have taken it with him.'

'Perhaps it will return and you can analyse the earth on its paws.'

'I'm not Lecoq, or even Maigret, and there's a war on.'

I went across to the bookcase and examined the two rows of books – Pyle's library. *The Advance of Red China, The Challenge to Democracy, The Rôle of the West* – these, I suppose, were the complete works of York Harding. There were a lot of Congressional Reports, a Vietnamese phrase book, a history of the War in the Philippines, a Modern Library Shakespeare. On what did he relax? I found his light reading on another shelf: a portable Thomas Wolfe and a

mysterious anthology called *The Triumph of Life* and a sel-
ection of American poetry. There was also a book of chess
problems. It didn't seem much for the end of the working day,
but, after all, he had had Phuong. Tucked away behind the
anthology there was a paper-backed book called *The Physiology of Marriage*. Perhaps he was studying sex, as he had
studied the East, on paper. And the keyword was marriage.
Pyle believed in being involved.

His desk was quite bare. 'You've made a clean sweep,' I
said.

'Oh,' Vigot said, 'I had to take charge of these on behalf
of the American Legation. You know how quickly rumour
spreads. There might have been looting. I had all his papers
sealed up.' He said it seriously without even smiling.

'Anything damaging?'

'We can't afford to find anything damaging against an ally,'
Vigot said.

'Would you mind if I took one of these books – as a
keepsake?'

'I'll look the other way.'

I chose York Harding's *The Rôle of the West* and packed
it in the box with Phuong's clothes.

'As a friend,' Vigot said, 'is there nothing you could tell
me in confidence? My report's all tied up. He was murdered
by the Communists. Perhaps the beginning of a campaign
against American aid. But between you and me – listen, it's
dry talking, what about a vermouth cassis round the corner?'

'Too early.'

'He didn't confide anything to you the last time he saw
you?'

'No.'

'When was that?'

'Yesterday morning. After the big bang.'

He paused to let my reply sink in – to my mind, not to his:
he interrogated fairly. 'You were out when he called on you
last night?'

'Last night? I must have been. I didn't think . . .'

'You may be wanting an exit visa. You know we could
delay it indefinitely.'

'Do you really believe,' I said, 'that I want to go home?'

Vigot looked through the window at the bright cloudless day. He said sadly, 'Most people do.'

'I like it here. At home there are – problems.'

'*Merde*,' Vigot said, 'here's the American Economic Attaché.' He repeated with sarcasm, 'Economic Attaché.'

'I'd better be off. He'll want to seal me up too.'

Vigot said wearily, 'I wish you luck. He'll have a terrible lot to say to me.'

The Economic Attaché was standing by his Packard when I came out, trying to explain something to his driver. He was a stout middle-aged man with an exaggerated bottom and a face that looked as if it never needed a razor. He called out, 'Fowler. Could you explain to this darned driver . . . ?'

I explained.

He said, 'But that's just what I told him, but he always pretends not to understand French.'

'It may be a matter of accent.'

'I was three years in Paris. My accent's good enough for one of these darned Vietnamese.'

'The voice of Democracy,' I said.

'What's that?'

'I expect it's a book by York Harding.'

'I don't get you.' He took a suspicious look at the box I carried. 'What've you got there?' he said.

'Two pairs of white silk trousers, two silk robes, some girl's underpants – three pairs, I think. All home products. No American aid.'

'Have you been up there?' he asked.

'Yes.'

'You heard the news?'

'Yes.'

'It's a terrible thing,' he said, 'terrible.'

'I expect the Minister's very disturbed.'

'I should say. He's with the High Commissioner now, and he's asked for an interview with the President.' He put his hand on my arm and walked me away from the cars. 'You knew young Pyle well, didn't you? I can't get over a thing like that happening to him. I knew his father. Professor Harold C. Pyle – you'll have heard of him?'

'No.'

'He's the world authority on underwater erosion. Didn't you see his picture on the cover of *Time* the other month?'

'Oh, I think I remember. A crumbling cliff in the background and gold-rimmed glasses in the foreground.'

'That's him. I had to draft the cable home. It was terrible. I loved that boy like he was my son.'

'That makes you closely related to his father.'

He turned his wet brown eyes on me. He said, 'What's getting you? That's not the way to talk when a fine young fellow . . .'

'I'm sorry,' I said. 'Death takes people in different ways.' Perhaps he had really loved Pyle. 'What did you say in your cable?' I asked.

He replied seriously and literally, '"Grieved to report your son died a soldier's death in cause of Democracy." The Minister signed it.'

'A soldier's death,' I said. 'Mightn't that prove a bit confusing? I mean to the folks at home. The Economic Aid Mission doesn't sound like the Army. Do you get Purple Hearts?'

He said in a low voice, tense with ambiguity, 'He had special duties.'

'Oh yes, we all guessed that.'

'He didn't talk, did he?'

'Oh no,' I said, and Vigot's phrase came back to me, 'He was a very quiet American.'

'Have you any hunch,' he asked, 'why they killed him? and who?'

Suddenly I was angry; I was tired of the whole pack of them with their private stores of Coca-Cola and their portable hospitals and their too wide cars and their not quite latest guns. I said, 'Yes. They killed him because he was too innocent to live. He was young and ignorant and silly and he got involved. He had no more of a notion than any of you what the whole affair's about, and you gave him money and York

31

Harding's books on the East and said, "Go ahead. Win the East for Democracy." He never saw anything he hadn't heard in a lecture-hall, and his writers and his lecturers made a fool of him. When he saw a dead body he couldn't even see the wounds. A Red menace, a soldier of democracy.'

'I thought you were his friend,' he said in a tone of reproach.

'I *was* his friend. I'd have liked to see him reading the Sunday supplements at home and following the baseball. I'd have liked to see him safe with a standardized American girl who subscribed to the Book Club.'

He cleared his throat with embarrassment. 'Of course,' he said, 'I'd forgotten that unfortunate business. I was quite on your side, Fowler. He behaved very badly. I don't mind telling you I had a long talk with him about the girl. You see, I had the advantage of knowing Professor and Mrs Pyle.'

I said, 'Vigot's waiting,' and walked away. For the first time he spotted Phuong and when I looked back at him he was watching me with pained perplexity: an eternal brother who didn't understand.

Chapter 3

1

THE first time Pyle met Phuong was again at the Continental, perhaps two months after his arrival. It was the early evening, in the momentary cool which came when the sun had just gone down, and the candles were lit on the stalls in the side streets. The dice rattled on the tables where the French were playing *Quatre Cent Vingt-et-un* and the girls in the white silk trousers bicycled home down the rue Catinat. Phuong was drinking a glass of orange juice and I was having a beer and we sat in silence, content to be together. Then Pyle came tentatively across, and I introduced them. He had a way of staring hard at a girl as though he hadn't seen one before and then blushing. 'I was wondering whether you and your lady,' Pyle said, 'would step across and join my table. One of our attachés . . .'

It was the Economic Attaché. He beamed down at us from the terrace above, a great warm welcoming smile, full of confidence, like the man who keeps his friends because he uses the right deodorants. I had heard him called Joe a number of times, but I had never learnt his surname. He made a noisy show of pulling out chairs and calling for the waiter, though all that activity could possibly produce at the Continental was a choice of beer, brandy-and-soda or vermouth cassis. 'Didn't expect to see you here, Fowler,' he said. 'We are waiting for the boys back from Hanoi. There seems to have been quite a battle. Weren't you with them?'

'I'm tired of flying four hours for a Press Conference,' I said.

He looked at me with disapproval. He said, 'These guys are real keen. Why, I expect they could earn twice as much in business or on the radio without any risk.'

'They might have to work,' I said.

'They seem to sniff the battle like war-horses,' he went on exultantly, paying no attention to words he didn't like. 'Bill Granger – you can't keep him out of a scrap.'

'I expect you're right. I saw him in one the other evening at the bar of the Sporting.'

'You know very well I didn't mean that.'

Two trishaw drivers came pedalling furiously down the rue Catinat and drew up in a photo-finish outside the Continental. In the first was Granger. The other contained a small, grey, silent heap which Granger now began to pull out on to the pavement. 'Oh, come on, Mick,' he said, 'come on.' Then he began to argue with his driver about the fare. 'Here,' he said, 'take it or leave it,' and flung five times the correct amount into the street for the man to stoop for.

The Economic Attaché said nervously, 'I guess these boys deserve a little relaxation.'

Granger flung his burden on to a chair. Then he noticed Phuong. 'Why,' he said, 'you old so-and-so, Joe. Where did you find her? Didn't know you had a whistle in you. Sorry, got to find the can. Look after Mick.'

'Rough soldierly manners,' I said.

Pyle said earnestly, blushing again, 'I wouldn't have invited you two over if I'd thought . . .'

The grey heap stirred in the chair and the head fell on the table as though it wasn't attached. It sighed, a long whistling sigh of infinite tedium, and lay still.

'Do you know him?' I asked Pyle.

'No. Isn't he one of the Press?'

'I heard Bill call him Mick,' the Economic Attaché said.

'Isn't there a new U.P. correspondent?'

'It's not him. I know him. What about your Economic Mission? You can't know all your people – there are hundreds of them.'

'I don't think he belongs,' the Economic Attaché said. 'I can't recollect him.'

'We might find his identity card,' Pyle suggested.

'For God's sake don't wake him. One drunk's enough. Anyway Granger will know.'

But he didn't. He came gloomily back from the lavatory. 'Who's the dame?' he asked morosely.

'Miss Phuong is a friend of Fowler's,' Pyle said stiffly. 'We want to know who . . .'

'Where'd he find her? You got to be careful in this town.' He added gloomily, 'Thank God for penicillin.'

'Bill,' the Economic Attaché said, 'we want to know who Mick is.'

'Search me.'

'But you brought him here.'

'The Frogs can't take Scotch. He passed out.'

'Is he French? I thought you called him Mick.'

'Had to call him something,' Granger said. He leant over to Phuong and said, 'Here. You. Have another glass of orange? Got a date tonight?'

I said, 'She's got a date every night.'

The Economic Attaché said hurriedly, 'How's the war, Bill?'

'Great victory north-west of Hanoi. French recaptured two villages they never told us they'd lost. Heavy Vietminh casualties. Haven't been able to count their own yet but will let us know in a week or two.'

The Economic Attaché said, 'There's a rumour that the Vietminh have broken into Phat Diem, burned the Cathedral, chased out the Bishop.'

'They wouldn't tell us about that in Hanoi. That's not a victory.'

'One of our medical teams couldn't get beyond Nam Dinh,' Pyle said.

'You didn't get down as far as that, Bill?' the Economic Attaché asked.

'Who do you think I am? I'm a correspondent with an *Ordre de Circulation* which shows when I'm out of bounds. I fly to Hanoi airport. They give us a car to the Press Camp. They lay on a flight over the two towns they've recaptured and show us the tricolour flying. It might be any darned flag at that height. Then we have a Press Conference and a colonel explains to us what we've been looking at. Then we file our cables with the censor. Then we have drinks. Best barman in Indo-China. Then we catch the plane back.'

Pyle frowned at his beer.

'You underrate yourself, Bill,' the Economic Attaché said. 'Why, that account of Road 66 – what did you call it? Highway to Hell – that was worthy of the Pulitzer. You know the story I mean – the man with his head blown off kneeling in the ditch, and that other you saw walking in a dream . . .'

'Do you think I'd really go near their stinking highway? Stephen Crane could describe a war without seeing one. Why shouldn't I? It's only a damned colonial war anyway. Get me another drink. And then let's go and find a girl. You've got a piece of tail. I want a piece of tail too.'

I said to Pyle, 'Do you think there's anything in the rumour about Phat Diem?'

'I don't know. Is it important? I'd like to go and have a look,' he said, 'if it's important.'

'Important to the Economic Mission?'

'Oh, well,' he said, 'you can't draw hard lines. Medicine's a kind of weapon, isn't it? These Catholics, they'd be pretty strong against the Communists, wouldn't they?'

'They trade with the Communists. The Bishop gets his cows and the bamboo for his building from the Communists. I wouldn't say they were exactly York Harding's Third Force,' I teased him.

'Break it up,' Granger was shouting. 'Can't waste the whole night here. I'm off to the House of Five Hundred Girls.'

'If you and Miss Phuong would have dinner with me . . .' Pyle said.

'You can eat at the Chalet,' Granger interrupted him, 'while I'm knocking the girls next door. Come on, Joe. Anyway you're a man.'

I think it was then, wondering what a man is, that I felt my first affection for Pyle. He sat a little turned away from Granger, twisting his beer mug, with an expression of determined remoteness. He said to Phuong, 'I guess you get tired of all this shop – about your country, I mean?'

'*Comment?*'

'What are you going to do with Mick?' the Economic Attaché asked.

'Leave him here,' Granger said.

'You can't do that. You don't even know his name.'

'We could bring him along and let the girls look after him.'

The Economic Attaché gave a loud communal laugh. He looked like a face on television. He said, 'You young people can do what you want, but I'm too old for games. I'll take him home with me. Did you say he was French?'

'He spoke French.'

'If you can get him into my car . . .'

After he had driven away, Pyle took a trishaw with Granger, and Phuong and I followed along the road to Cholon. Granger had made an attempt to get into the trishaw with Phuong, but Pyle diverted him. As they pedalled us down the long suburban road to the Chinese town a line of French armoured cars went by, each with its jutting gun and silent officer motionless like a figurehead under the stars and the black, smooth, concave sky – trouble again probably with a private army, the Binh Xuyen, who ran the Grand Monde and the gambling halls of Cholon. This was a land of rebellious barons. It was like Europe in the Middle Ages. But what were the Americans doing here? Columbus had not yet discovered their country. I said to Phuong, 'I like that fellow, Pyle.'

'He's quiet,' she said, and the adjective which she was the first to use stuck like a schoolboy name, till I heard even Vigot use it, sitting there with his green eye-shade, telling me of Pyle's death.

I stopped our trishaw outside the Chalet and said to Phuong, 'Go in and find a table. I had better look after Pyle.' That was my first instinct – to protect him. It never occurred to me that there was greater need to protect myself. Innocence always calls mutely for protection when we would be so much wiser to guard ourselves against it: innocence is like a dumb leper who has lost his bell, wandering the world, meaning no harm.

When I reached the House of the Five Hundred Girls, Pyle and Granger had gone inside. I asked at the military police post just inside the doorway, *'Deux Américains?'*

He was a young Foreign Legion corporal. He stopped cleaning his revolver and jutted his thumb towards the doorway beyond, making a joke in German. I couldn't understand it.

It was the hour of rest in the immense courtyard which lay open to the sky. Hundreds of girls lay on the grass or sat on their heels talking to their companions. The curtains were undrawn in the little cubicles around the square – one tired girl lay alone on a bed with her ankles crossed. There was trouble in Cholon and the troops were confined to quarters and there was no work to be done: the Sunday of the body. Only a knot of fighting, scrabbling, shouting girls showed me where custom was still alive. I remembered the old Saigon story of the distinguished visitor who had lost his trousers fighting his way back to the safety of the police post. There was no protection here for the civilian. If he chose to poach on military territory, he must look after himself and find his own way out.

I had learnt a technique – to divide and conquer. I chose one in the crowd that gathered round me and edged her slowly towards the spot where Pyle and Granger struggled.

'Je suis un vieux,' I said. *'Trop fatigué.'* She giggled and pressed. *'Mon ami.'* I said, *'il est très riche, très vigoureux.'*

'Tu es sale,' she said.

I caught sight of Granger flushed and triumphant; it was as though he took this demonstration as a tribute to his manhood. One girl had her arm through Pyle's and was trying to tug him gently out of the ring. I pushed my girl in among them and called to him, 'Pyle, over here.'

He looked at me over their heads and said, 'It's terrible. Terrible.' It may have been a trick of the lamplight, but his face looked haggard. It occurred to me that he was quite possibly a virgin.

'Come along, Pyle,' I said. 'Leave them to Granger.' I saw his hand move towards his hip pocket. I really believe he intended to empty his pockets of piastres and greenbacks. 'Don't be a fool, Pyle,' I called sharply. 'You'll have them fighting.' My girl was turning back to me and I gave her another push into the inner ring round Granger. *'Non, non,'* I said, *'je suis un Anglais, pauvre, très pauvre.'* Then I got hold of Pyle's sleeve and dragged him out, with the girl hanging on to his other arm like a hooked fish. Two or three girls tried to intercept us before we got to the gateway where the corporal stood watching, but they were half-hearted.

'What'll I do with this one?' Pyle said.

38

'She won't be any trouble,' and at that moment she let go his arm and dived back into the scrimmage round Granger.

'Will he be all right?' Pyle asked anxiously.

'He's got what he wanted – a bit of tail.'

The night outside seemed very quiet with only another squadron of armoured cars driving by like people with a purpose. He said, 'It's terrible. I wouldn't have believed . . .' He said with sad awe, 'They were so pretty.' He was not envying Granger, he was complaining that anything good – and prettiness and grace are surely forms of goodness – should be marred or ill-treated. Pyle could see pain when it was in front of his eyes. (I don't write that as a sneer; after all there are many of us who can't.)

I said, 'Come back to the Chalet. Phuong's waiting.'

'I'm sorry,' he said. 'I quite forgot. You shouldn't have left her.'

'*She* wasn't in danger.'

'I just thought I'd see Granger safely . . .' He dropped again into his thoughts, but as we entered the Chalet he said with obscure distress, 'I'd forgotten how many men there are . . .'

2

Phuong had kept us a table at the edge of the dance-floor and the orchestra was playing some tune which had been popular in Paris five years ago. Two Vietnamese couples were dancing, small, neat, aloof, with an air of civilization we couldn't match. (I recognized one, an accountant from the Banque de l'Indo-Chine and his wife.) They never, one felt, dressed carelessly, said the wrong word, were a prey to untidy passion. If the war seemed medieval, they were like the eighteenth-century future. One would have expected Mr Pham-Van-Tu to write Augustans in his spare time, but I happened to know he was a student of Wordsworth and wrote nature poems. His holidays he spent at Dalat, the nearest he could get to the atmosphere of the English lakes. He bowed slightly as he came round. I wondered how Granger had fared fifty yards up the road.

Pyle was apologizing to Phuong in bad French for having kept her waiting. *'C'est impardonable,'* he said.

'Where have you been?' she asked him.

He said, 'I was seeing Granger home.'

'Home?' I said and laughed, and Pyle looked at me as though I were another Granger. Suddenly I saw myself as he saw me, a man of middle age, with eyes a little bloodshot, beginning to put on weight, ungraceful in love, less noisy than Granger perhaps but more cynical, less innocent, and I saw Phuong for a moment as I had seen her first, dancing past my table at the Grand Monde in a white ball-dress, eighteen years old, watched by an elder sister who had been determined on a good European marriage. An American had bought a ticket and asked her for a dance: he was a little drunk – not harmfully, and I suppose he was new to the country and thought the hostesses of the Grand Monde were whores. He held her much too close as they went round the floor the first time, and then suddenly there she was, going back to sit with her sister, and he was left, stranded and lost among the dancers, not knowing what had happened or why. And the girl whose name I didn't know sat quietly there, occasionally sipping her orange juice, owning herself completely.

'Peut-on avoir l'honneur?' Pyle was saying in his terrible accent, and a moment later I saw them dancing in silence at the other end of the room, Pyle holding her so far away from him that you expected him at any moment to sever contact. He was a very bad dancer, and she had been the best dancer I had ever known in her days at the Grand Monde.

It had been a long and frustrating courtship. If I could have offered marriage and a settlement everything would have been easy, and the elder sister would have slipped quietly and tactfully away whenever we were together. But three months passed before I saw her so much as momentarily alone, on a balcony at the Majestic, while her sister in the next room kept on asking when we proposed to come in. A cargo boat from France was being unloaded in Saigon River by the light of flares, the trishaw bells rang like telephones, and I might have been a young and inexperienced fool for all I found to say. I went back hopelessly to my bed in the rue Catinat and never

40

dreamed that four months later she would be lying beside me, a little out of breath, laughing as though with surprise because nothing had been quite what she expected.

'Monsieur Fowlair.' I had been watching them dance and hadn't seen her sister signalling to me from another table. Now she came over and I reluctantly asked her to sit down. We had never been friends since the night she was taken ill in the Grand Monde and I had seen Phuong home.

'I haven't seen you for a whole year,' she said.

'I am away so often at Hanoi.'

'Who is your friend?' she asked.

'A man called Pyle.'

'What does he do?'

'He belongs to the American Economic Mission. You know the kind of thing – electrical sewing machines for starving seamstresses.'

'Are there any?'

'I don't know.'

'But they don't use sewing machines. There wouldn't be any electricity where they live.' She was a very literal woman.

'You'll have to ask Pyle,' I said.

'Is he married?'

I looked at the dance floor. 'I should say that's as near as he ever got to a woman.'

'He dances very badly,' she said.

'Yes.'

'But he looks a nice reliable man.'

'Yes.'

'Can I sit with you for a little? My friends are very dull.'

The music stopped and Pyle bowed stiffly to Phuong, then led her back and drew out her chair. I could tell that his formality pleased her. I thought how much she missed in her relation to me.

'This is Phuong's sister,' I said to Pyle. 'Miss Hei.'

'I'm very glad to meet you,' he said and blushed.

'You come from New York?' she asked.

'No. From Boston.'

'That is in the United States too?'

'Oh yes. Yes.'

'Is your father a business man?'

'Not really. He's a professor.'

'A teacher?' she asked with a faint note of disappointment.

'Well, he's a kind of authority, you know. People consult him.'

'About health? Is he a doctor?'

'Not that sort of doctor. He's a doctor of engineering though. He understands all about underwater erosion. You know what that is?'

'No.'

Pyle said with a dim attempt at humour, 'Well, I'll leave it to Dad to tell you about that.'

'He is here?'

'Oh no.'

'But he is coming?'

'No. That was just a joke,' Pyle said apologetically.

'Have you got another sister?' I asked Miss Hei.

'No. Why?'

'It sounds as though you were examining Mr Pyle's marriageability.'

'I have only one sister,' Miss Hei said, and she clamped her hand heavily down on Phuong's knee, like a chairman with his gravel marking a point of order.

'She's a very pretty sister,' Pyle said.

'She is the most beautiful girl in Saigon,' Miss Hei said, as though she were correcting him.

'I can believe it.'

I said, 'It's time we ordered dinner. Even the most beautiful girl in Saigon must eat.'

'I am not hungry,' Phuong said.

'She is delicate,' Miss Hei went firmly on. There was a note of menace in her voice. 'She needs care. She deserves care. She is very, very loyal.'

'My friend is a lucky man,' Pyle said gravely.

'She loves children,' Miss Hei said.

I laughed and then caught Pyle's eye; he was looking at me with shocked surprise, and suddenly it occurred to me that he was genuinely interested in what Miss Hei had to say. While I was ordering dinner (though Phuong had told me she was

42

not hungry, I knew she could manage a good steak tartare with two raw eggs and etceteras), I listened to him seriously discussing the question of children. 'I've always thought I'd like a lot of children,' he said. 'A big family's a wonderful interest. It makes for the stability of marriage. And it's good for the children too. I was an only child. It's a great disadvantage being an only child.' I had never heard him talk so much before.

'How old is your father?' Miss Hei asked with gluttony.

'Sixty-nine.'

'Old people love grandchildren. It is very sad that my sister has no parents to rejoice in her children. When the day comes,' she added with a baleful look at me.

'Nor you either,' Pyle said, rather unnecessarily I thought.

'Our father was of a very good family. He was a mandarin in Hué.'

I said, 'I've ordered dinner for all of you.'

'Not for me,' Miss Hei said. 'I must be going to my friends. I would like to meet Mr Pyle again. Perhaps you could manage that.'

'When I get back from the north,' I said.

'Are you going to the north?'

'I think it's time I had a look at the war.'

'But the Press are all back,' Pyle said.

'That's the best time for me. I don't have to meet Granger.'

'Then you must come and have dinner with me and my sister when Monsieur Fowlair is gone.' She added with morose courtesy, 'To cheer her up.'

After she had gone Pyle said, 'What a very nice cultivated woman. And she spoke English so well.'

'Tell him my sister was in business once in Singapore,' Phuong said proudly.

'Really? What kind of business?'

I translated for her. 'Import, export. She can do shorthand.'

'I wish we had more like her in the Economic Mission.'

'I will speak to her,' Phuong said. 'She would like to work for the Americans.'

After dinner they danced again. I am a bad dancer too and I hadn't the unselfconsciousness of Pyle – or had I possessed it, I wondered, in the days when I was first in love with Phuong? There must have been many occasions at the Grand Monde before the memorable night of Miss Hei's illness when I had danced with Phuong just for an opportunity to speak to her. Pyle was taking no such opportunity as they came round the floor again; he had relaxed a little, that was all, and was holding her less at arm's length, but they were both silent. Suddenly watching her feet, so light and precise and mistress of his shuffle, I was in love again. I could hardly believe that in an hour, two hours, she would be coming back to me to that dingy room with the communal closet and the old women squatting on the landing.

I wished I had never heard the rumour about Phat Diem, or that the rumour had dealt with any other town than the one place in the north where my friendship with a French naval officer would allow me to slip in, uncensored, uncontrolled. A newspaper scoop? Not in those days when all the world wanted to read about was Korea. A chance of death? Why should I want to die when Phuong slept beside me every night? But I knew the answer to that question. From childhood I had never believed in permanence, and yet I had longed for it. Always I was afraid of losing happiness. This month, next year, Phuong would leave me. If not next year, in three years. Death was the only absolute value in my world. Lose life and one would lose nothing again for ever. I envied those who could believe in a God and I distrusted them. I felt they were keeping their courage up with a fable of the changeless and the permanent. Death was far more certain than God, and with death there would be no longer the daily possibility of love dying. The nightmare of a future of boredom and indifference would lift. I could never have been a pacifist. To kill a man was surely to grant him an immeasurable benefit. Oh yes, people always, everywhere, loved their enemies. It was their friends they preserved for pain and vacuity.

'Forgive me for taking Miss Phuong from you,' Pyle's voice said.

'Oh, I'm no dancer, but I like watching her dance.' One

44

always spoke of her like that in the third person as though she were not there. Sometimes she seemed invisible like peace.

The first cabaret of the evening began: a singer, a juggler, a comedian – he was very obscene, but when I looked at Pyle he obviously couldn't follow the argot. He smiled when Phuong smiled and laughed uneasily when I laughed. 'I wonder where Granger is now,' I said, and Pyle looked at me reproachfully.

Then came the turn of the evening: a troupe of female impersonators. I had seen many of them during the day in the rue Catinat walking up and down, in old slacks and sweaters, a bit blue about the chin, swaying their hips. Now in low-cut evening dresses, with false jewellery and false breasts and husky voices, they appeared at least as desirable as most of the European women in Saigon. A group of young Air Force officers whistled to them and they smiled glamorously back. I was astonished by the sudden violence of Pyle's protest. 'Fowler,' he said, 'let's go. We've had enough, haven't we? This isn't a bit suitable for *her*.'

Chapter 4

1

FROM the bell tower of the Cathedral the battle was only picturesque, fixed like a panorama of the Boer War in an old *Illustrated London News*. An aeroplane was parachuting supplies to an isolated post in the *calcaire,* those strange weather-eroded mountains on the Annam border that look like piles of pumice, and because it always returned to the same place for its glide, it might never have moved, and the parachute was always there in the same spot, half-way to earth. From the plain the mortar-bursts rose unchangingly, the smoke as solid as stone, and in the market the flames burnt palely in the sunlight. The tiny figures of the parachutists moved in single file along the canals, but at this height they appeared stationary. Even the priest who sat in a corner of the tower never changed his position as he read in his breviary. The war was very tidy and clean at that distance.

I had come in before dawn in a landing-craft from Nam Dinh. We couldn't land at the naval station because it was cut off by the enemy who completely surrounded the town at a range of six hundred yards, so the boat ran in beside the flaming market. We were an easy target in the light of the flames, but for some reason no one fired. Everything was quiet, except for the flop and crackle of the burning stalls. I could hear a Senegalese sentry on the river's edge shift his stance.

I had known Phat Diem well in the days before the attack – the one long narrow street of wooden stalls, cut up every hundred yards by a canal, a church and a bridge. At night it had been lit only by candles or small oil lamps (there was no electricity in Phat Diem except in the French officers' quarters), and day or night the street was packed and noisy. In its strange medieval way, under the shadow and protection of the Prince Bishop, it had been the most living town in all the country, and now when I landed and walked up to the officers' quarters it was the most dead. Rubble and broken glass and the smell of burnt paint and plaster, the long street empty as far as the sight could reach, it reminded me of a London thoroughfare in the early morning after an all-clear: one expected to see a placard, 'Unexploded Bomb'.

The front wall of the officers' house had been blown out, and the houses across the street were in ruins. Coming down the river from Nam Dinh I had learnt from Lieutenant Peraud what had happened. He was a serious young man, a Freemason, and to him it was like a judgement on the superstitions of his fellows. The Bishop of Phat Diem had once visited Europe and acquired there a devotion to Our Lady of Fatima – that vision of the Virgin which appeared, so Roman Catholics believe, to a group of children in Portugal. When he came home, he built a grotto in her honour in the Cathedral precincts, and he celebrated her feast-day every year with a procession. Relations with the colonel in charge of the French and Vietnamese troops had always been strained since the day when the authorities had disbanded the Bishop's private army. This year the colonel – who had some sympathy with the Bishop, for to each of them his country was more important than Catholicism – made a gesture of amity and walked with his senior officers in the front of the procession. Never had a greater crowd gathered in Phat Diem to do honour to Our Lady of Fatima. Even many of the Buddhists – who formed about half the population – could not bear to miss the fun, and those who had belief in neither God nor Buddha believed that somehow all these banners and incense-burners and the golden monstrance would keep war from their homes. All that was left of the Bishop's army – his brass band – led the procession, and the French officers, pious by order of the colonel, followed like choirboys through the gateway into the Cathedral precincts, past the white statue of the Sacred Heart that stood on an island in the little lake before the Cathedral, under the bell tower with spreading oriental wings and into the carved wooden Cathedral with its gigantic pillars formed out of single trees and the scarlet lacquer work of the altar, more Buddhist than Christian. From all the villages between the canals, from that Low Country landscape where young green rice-shoots and golden harvests take the place of tulips and churches of windmills, the people poured in.

Nobody noticed the Vietminh agents who had joined the procession too, and that night as the main Communist battalion moved through the passes in the *calcaire*, into the Tonkin plain, watched helplessly by the French outpost in the mountains above, the advance agents struck in Phat Diem.

Now after four days, with the help of parachutists, the enemy had been pushed back half a mile around the town. This was a defeat: no journalists were allowed, no cables could be sent, for the papers must carry only victories. The authorities would have stopped me in Hanoi if they had known of my purpose, but the further you get from headquarters, the looser becomes the control until, when you come within range of the enemy's fire, you are a welcome guest – what has been a menace for the *Etat Major* in Hanoi, a worry for the full colonel in Nam Dinh, to the lieutenant in the field is a joke, a distraction, a mark of interest from the outer world, so that for a few blessed hours he can dramatize himself a little and see in a false heroic light even his own wounded and dead.

The priest shut his breviary and said, 'Well, that's finished.' He was a European, but not a Frenchman, for the Bishop would not have tolerated a French priest in his diocese. He said apologetically, 'I have to come up here, you understand, for a bit of quiet from all those poor people.' The sound of the mortar-fire seemed to be closing in, or perhaps it was the enemy at last replying. The strange difficulty was to find them: there were a dozen narrow fronts, and between the canals, among the farm buildings and the paddy fields, innumerable opportunities for ambush.

Immediately below us stood, sat and lay the whole population of Phat Diem. Catholics, Buddhists, pagans, they had all packed their most valued possessions – a cooking-stove, a lamp, a mirror, a wardrobe, some mats, a holy picture – and moved into the Cathedral precincts. Here in the north it would be bitterly cold when darkness came, and already the Cathedral was full: there was no more shelter; even on the stairs to the bell tower every step was occupied, and all the time more people crowded through the gates, carrying their babies and household goods. They believed, whatever their religion, that here they would be safe. While we watched, a young man with a rifle in Vietnamese uniform pushed his way through: he was stopped by a priest, who took his rifle from him. The father at my side said in explanation, 'We are neutral here. This is God's territory.' I thought, 'It's a strange poor population God has in his kingdom, frightened, cold, starving – "I don't know how we are going to feed these people," the priest told me – you'd think a great King would do better than that.' But then I thought, 'It's always the same wherever one goes – it's not the most powerful rulers who have the happiest populations.'

Little shops had already been set up below. I said, 'It's like an enormous fair, isn't it, but without one smiling face.'

The priest said, 'They were terribly cold last night. We have to keep the monastery gates shut or they would swamp us.'

'You all keep warm in here?' I asked.

'Not very warm. And we would not have room for a tenth of them.' He went on, 'I know what you are thinking. But it is essential for some of us to keep well. We have the only hospital in Phat Diem, and our only nurses are these nuns.'

'And your surgeon?'

'I do what I can.' I saw then that his soutane was speckled with blood.

He said, 'Did you come up here to find me?'

'No. I wanted to get my bearings.'

'I asked you because I had a man up here last night. He wanted to go to confession. He had got a little frightened, you see, with what he had seen along the canal. One couldn't blame him.'

'It's bad along there?'

'The parachutists caught them in a cross-fire. Poor souls. I thought perhaps you were feeling the same.'

'I'm not a Roman Catholic. I don't think you could even call me a Christian.'

'It's strange what fear does to a man.'

'It would never do that to me. If I believed in any God at

49

all, I should still hate the idea of confession. Kneeling in one of your boxes. Exposing myself to another man. You must excuse me, Father, but to me it seems morbid – unmanly even.'

'Oh,' he said lightly, 'I expect you are a good man. I don't suppose you've ever had much to regret.'

I looked along the churches, where they ran down evenly spaced between the canals, towards the sea. A light flashed from the second tower. I said, 'You haven't kept all your churches neutral.'

'It isn't possible,' he said. 'The French have agreed to leave the Cathedral precincts alone. We can't expect more. That's a Foreign Legion post you are looking at.'

'I'll be going along. Good-bye, Father.'

'Good-bye and good luck. Be careful of the snipers.'

I had to push my way through the crowd to get out, past the lake and the white statue with its sugary outspread arms, into the long street. I could see for nearly three quarters of a mile each way, and there were only two living beings in all that length besides myself – two soldiers with camouflaged helmets going slowly away up the edge of the street, their sten guns at the ready. I say the living because one body lay in a doorway with its head in the road. The buzz of flies collecting there and the squelch of the soldiers' boots growing fainter and fainter were the only sounds. I walked quickly past the body, turning my head the other way. A few minutes later when I looked back I was quite alone with my shadow and there were no sounds except the sounds I made. I felt as though I were a mark on a firing range. It occurred to me that if something happened to me in this street it might be many hours before I was picked up: time for the flies to collect.

When I had crossed two canals, I took a turning that led to a church. A dozen men sat on the ground in the camouflage of parachutists, while two officers examined a map. Nobody paid me any attention when I joined them. One man, who wore the long antennae of a walkie-talkie, said, 'We can move now,' and everybody stood up.

I asked them in my bad French whether I could accompany

them. An advantage of this war was that a European face proved in itself a passport on the field: a European could not be suspected of being an enemy agent. 'Who are you?' the lieutenant asked.

'I am writing about the war,' I said.

'American?'

'No, English.'

He said, 'It is a very small affair, but if you wish to come with us ...' He began to take off his steel helmet. 'No, no,' I said, 'that is for combatants.'

'As you wish.'

We went out behind the church in single file, the lieutenant leading, and halted for a moment on a canal-bank for the soldier with the walkie-talkie to get contact with the patrols on either flank. The mortar shells tore over us and burst out of sight. We had picked up more men behind the church and were now about thirty strong. The lieutenant explained to me in a low voice, stabbing a finger at his map, 'Three hundred have been reported in this village here. Perhaps massing for tonight. We don't know. No one has found them yet.'

'How far?'

'Three hundred yards.'

Words came over the wireless and we went on in silence, to the right the straight canal, to the left low scrub and fields and scrub again. 'All clear,' the lieutenant whispered with a re-assuring wave as we started. Forty yards on, another canal, with what was left of a bridge, a single plank without rails, ran across our front. The lieutenant motioned to us to deploy and we squatted down facing the unknown territory ahead, thirty feet off, across the plank. The men looked at the water and then, as though by a word of command, all together, they looked away. For a moment I didn't see what they had seen, but when I saw, my mind went back, I don't know why, to the Chalet and the female impersonators and the young soldiers whistling and Pyle saying, 'This isn't a bit suitable.'

The canal was full of bodies: I am reminded now of an Irish stew containing too much meat. The bodies overlapped: one head, seal-grey, and anonymous as a convict with a shaven scalp, stuck up out of the water like a buoy. There was

no blood: I suppose it had flowed away a long time ago. I
have no idea how many there were: they must have been
caught in a cross-fire, trying to get back, and I suppose every
man of us along the bank was thinking, 'Two can play at
that game.' I too took my eyes away; we didn't want to be
reminded of how little we counted, how quickly, simply and
anonymously death came. Even though my reason wanted the
state of death, I was afraid like a virgin of the act. I would
have liked death to come with due warning, so that I could
prepare myself. For what? I didn't know, nor how, except by
taking a look around at the little I would be leaving.

The lieutenant sat beside the man with the walkie-talkie and
stared at the ground between his feet. The instrument began
to crackle instructions and with a sigh as though he had been
roused from sleep he got up. There was an odd comradeliness
about all their movements, as though they were equals engaged on a task they had performed together times out of
mind. Nobody waited to be told what to do. Two men made
for the plank and tried to cross it, but they were unbalanced
by the weight of their arms and had to sit astride and work
their way across a few inches at a time. Another man had
found a punt hidden in some bushes down the canal and he
worked it to where the lieutenant stood. Six of us got in and
he began to pole towards the other bank, but we ran on a
shoal of bodies and stuck. He pushed away with his pole,
sinking it into this human clay, and one body was released
and floated up all its length beside the boat like a bather lying
in the sun. Then we were free again, and once on the other
side we scrambled out, with no backward look. No shots had
been fired: we were alive: death had withdrawn perhaps as
far as the next canal. I heard somebody just behind me say
with great seriousness, '*Gott sei dank.*' Except for the lieutenant they were most of them Germans.

Beyond was a group of farm-buildings; the lieutenant went
in first, hugging the wall, and we followed at six-foot intervals
in single file. Then the men, again without an order, scattered
through the farm. Life had deserted it – not so much as a hen
had been left behind, though hanging on the walls of what
had been the living room where two hideous oleographs of the

Sacred Heart and the Mother and Child which gave the whole ramshackle group of buildings a European air. One knew what these people believed even if one didn't share their belief: they were human beings, not just grey drained cadavers.

So much of the war is sitting around and doing nothing, waiting for somebody else. With no guarantee of the amount of time you have left it doesn't seem worth starting even a train of thought. Doing what they had done so often before, the sentries moved out. Anything that stirred ahead of us now was enemy. The lieutenant marked his map and reported our position over the radio. A noonday hush fell: even the mortars were quiet and the air was empty of planes. One man doodled with a twig in the dirt of the farmyard. After a while it was as if we had been forgotten by war. I hoped that Phuong had sent my suits to the cleaners. A cold wind ruffled the straw of the yard, and a man went modestly behind a barn to relieve himself. I tried to remember whether I had paid the British Consul in Hanoi for the bottle of whisky he had allowed me.

Two shots were fired to our front, and I thought, 'This is it. Now it comes.' It was all the warning I wanted. I awaited, with a sense of exhilaration, the permanent thing.

But nothing happened. Once again I had 'over-prepared the event'. Only long minutes afterwards one of the sentries entered and reported something to the lieutenant. I caught the phrase, '*Deux civils.*'

The lieutenant said to me, 'We will go and see,' and following the sentry we picked our way along a muddy overgrown path between two fields. Twenty yards beyond the farm buildings, in a narrow ditch, we came on what we sought: a woman and a small boy. They were very clearly dead: a small neat clot of blood on the woman's forehead, and the child might have been sleeping. He was about six years old and he lay like an embryo in the womb with his little bony knees drawn up. '*Mal chance,*' the lieutenant said. He bent down and turned the child over. He was wearing a holy medal round his neck, and I said to myself, 'The juju doesn't work.' There was a gnawed piece of loaf under his body. I thought, 'I hate war.'

The lieutenant said, 'Have you seen enough?' speaking

savagely, almost as though I had been responsible for these deaths. Perhaps to the soldier the civilian is the man who employs him to kill, who includes the guilt of murder in the pay-envelope and escapes responsibility. We walked back to the farm and sat down again in silence on the straw, out of the wind, which like an animal seemed to know that dark was coming. The man who had doodled was relieving himself, and the man who had relieved himself was doodling. I thought how in those moments of quiet, after the sentries had been posted, they must have believed it safe to move from the ditch. I wondered whether they had lain there long – the bread had been very dry. This farm was probably their home.

The radio was working again. The lieutenant said wearily, 'They are going to bomb the village. Patrols are called in for the night.' We rose and began our journey back, punting again around the shoal of bodies, filing past the church. We hadn't gone very far, and yet it seemed a long enough journey to have made with the killing of those two as the only result. The planes had gone up, and behind us the bombing began.

Dark had fallen by the time I reached the officers' quarters, where I was spending the night. The temperature was only a degree above zero, and the sole warmth anywhere was in the blazing market. With one wall destroyed by a bazooka and the doors buckled, canvas curtains couldn't shut out the draughts. The electric dynamo was not working, and we had to build barricades of boxes and books to keep the candles burning. I played Quatre Cent Vingt-et-un for Communist currency with a Captain Sorel: it wasn't possible to play for drinks as I was a guest of the mess. The luck went wearisomely back and forth. I opened my bottle of whisky to try to warm us a little, and the others gathered round. The colonel said, 'This is the first glass of whisky I have had since I left Paris.'

A lieutenant came in from his round of the sentries. 'Perhaps we shall have a quiet night,' he said.

'They will not attack before four,' the colonel said. 'Have you a gun?' he asked me.

'No.'

'I'll find you one. Better keep it on your pillow.' He added courteously, 'I am afraid you will find your mattress rather hard. And at three-thirty the mortar-fire will begin. We try to break up any concentrations.'

'How long do you suppose this will go on?'

'Who knows? We can't spare any more troops from Nam Dinh. This is just a diversion. If we can hold out with no more help than we got two days ago, it is, one may say, a victory.'

The wind was up again, prowling for an entry. The canvas curtain sagged (I was reminded of Polonius stabbed behind the arras) and the candle wavered. The shadows were theatrical. We might have been a company of barnstormers.

'Have your posts held?'

'As far as we know.' He said with an effect of great tiredness, 'This is nothing, you understand, an affair of no importance compared with what is happening a hundred kilometres away at Hoa Binh. That is a battle.'

'Another glass, Colonel?'

'Thank you, no. It is wonderful, your English whisky, but it is better to keep a little for the night in case of need. I think, if you will excuse me, I will get some sleep. One cannot sleep after the mortars start. Captain Sorel, you will see that Monsieur Fowlair has everything he needs, a candle, matches, a revolver.' He went into his room.

It was the signal for all of us. They had put a mattress on the floor for me in a small store-room and I was surrounded by wooden cases. I stayed awake only a very short time – the hardness of the floors was like rest. I wondered, but oddly without jealousy, whether Phuong was at the flat. The possession of a body tonight seemed a very small thing – perhaps that day I had seen too many bodies which belonged to no one, not even to themselves. We were all expendable. When I fell asleep I dreamed of Pyle. He was dancing all by himself on a stage, stiffly, with his arms held out to an invisible partner, and I sat and watched him from a seat like a music-stool with a gun in my hand in case anyone should interfere with his dance. A programme set up by the stage, like the numbers in an English music-hall, read, 'The Dance of Love "A" certificate.' Somebody moved at the back of the theatre and I held my gun tighter. Then I woke.

My hand was on the gun they had lent me, and a man stood in the doorway with a candle in his hand. He wore a steel helmet which threw a shadow over his eyes, and it was only when he spoke that I knew he was Pyle. He said shyly, 'I'm awfully sorry to wake you up. They told me I could sleep in here.'

I was still not fully awake. 'Where did you get that helmet?' I asked.

'Oh, somebody lent it to me,' he said vaguely. He dragged in after him a military kitbag and began to pull out a wool-lined sleeping-bag.

'You are very well equipped,' I said, trying to recollect why either of us should be here.

'This is the standard travelling kit,' he said, 'of our medical aid teams. They lent me one in Hanoi.' He took out a thermos and a small spirit stove, a hair-brush, a shaving-set and a tin of rations. I looked at my watch. It was nearly three in the morning.

2

Pyle continued to unpack. He made a little ledge of cases, on which he put his shaving-mirror and tackle. I said, 'I doubt if you'll get any water.'

'Oh,' he said, 'I've enough in the thermos for the morning.' He sat down on his sleeping-bag and began to pull off his boots.

'How on earth did you get here?' I asked.

'They let me through as far as Nam Dinh to see our trachoma team, and then I hired a boat.'

'A boat?'

'Oh, some kind of a punt – I don't know the name for it. As a matter of fact I had to buy it. It didn't cost much.'

'And you came down the river by yourself?'

'It wasn't really difficult, you know. The current was with me.'

'You are crazy.'

'Oh no. The only real danger was running aground.'

'Or being shot up by a naval patrol, or a French plane. Or having your throat cut by the Vietminh.'

He laughed shyly. 'Well, I'm here anyway,' he said.

'Why?'

'Oh, there are two reasons. But I don't want to keep you awake.'

'I'm not sleepy. The guns will be starting soon.'

'Do you mind if I move the candle? It's a little too bright here.' He seemed nervous.

'What's the first reason?'

'Well, the other day you made me think this place was rather interesting. You remember when we were with Granger . . . and Phuong.'

'Yes?'

'I thought I ought to take a look at it. To tell you the truth, I was a little ashamed of Granger.'

'I see. As simple as all that.'

'Well, there wasn't any real difficulty, was there?' He began to play with his bootlaces, and there was a long silence. 'I'm not being quite honest,' he said at last.

'No?'

'I really came to see you.'

'You came here to see me?'

'Yes.'

'Why?'

He looked up from his bootlaces in an agony of embarrassment. 'I had to tell you – I've fallen in love with Phuong.'

I laughed. I couldn't help it. He was so unexpected and serious. I said, 'Couldn't you have waited till I got back? I shall be in Saigon next week.'

'You might have been killed,' he said. 'It wouldn't have been honourable. And then I don't know if I could have stayed away from Phuong all that time.'

'You mean, you *have* stayed away?'

'Of course. You don't think I'll tell *her* – without you knowing?'

'People do,' I said. 'When did it happen?'

'I guess it was that night at the Chalet, dancing with her.'

'I didn't think you ever got close enough.'

He looked at me in a puzzled way. If his conduct seemed crazy to me, mine was obviously inexplicable to him. He said,

'You know, I think it was seeing all those girls in that house. They were so pretty. Why, she might have been one of them. I wanted to protect her.'

'I don't think she's in need of protection. Has Miss Hei invited you out?'

'Yes, but I haven't gone. I've kept away.' He said gloomily, 'It's been terrible. I feel such a heel, but you do believe me, don't you, that if you'd been married – why, I wouldn't ever come between a man and his wife.'

'You seem pretty sure you *can* come between,' I said. For the first time he had irritated me.

'Fowler,' he said, 'I don't know your Christian name . . . ?'

'Thomas. Why?'

'I can call you Tom, can't I? I feel in a way this has brought us together. Loving the same woman, I mean.'

'What's your next move?'

He sat up enthusiastically against the packing-cases. 'Everything seems different now that you know,' he said. 'I shall ask her to marry me, Tom.'

'I'd rather you called me Thomas.'

'She'll just have to choose between us, Thomas. That's fair enough.' But was it fair? I felt for the first time the premonitory chill of loneliness. It was all fantastic, and yet . . . He might be a poor lover, but I was the poor man. He had in his hand the infinite riches of respectability.

He began to undress and I thought, 'He has youth too.' How sad it was to envy Pyle.

I said, 'I can't marry her. I have a wife at home. She would never divorce me. She's High Church – if you know what that means.'

'I'm sorry, Thomas. By the way, my name's Alden, if you'd care . . .'

'I'd rather stick to Pyle,' I said. 'I think of you as Pyle.'

He got into his sleeping-bag and stretched his hand out for the candle. 'Whew,' he said, 'I'm glad that's over, Thomas. I've been feeling awfully bad about it.' It was only too evident that he no longer did.

When the candle was out, I could just see the outline of his crew-cut against the light of the flames outside. 'Goodnight,

Thomas. Sleep well,' and immediately at those words like a bad comedy cue the mortars opened up, whirring, shrieking, exploding.

'Good God,' Pyle said, 'is it an attack?'

'They are trying to stop an attack.'

'Well, I suppose, there'll be no sleep for us now?'

'No sleep.'

'Thomas, I want you to know what I think of the way you've taken all this – I think you've been swell, swell, there's no other word for it.'

'Thank you.'

'You've seen so much more of the world than I have. You know, in some ways Boston is a bit – cramping. Even if you aren't a Lowell or a Cabot. I wish you'd advise me, Thomas.'

'What about?'

'Phuong.'

'I wouldn't trust my advice if I were you. I'm biased. I want to keep her.'

'Oh, but I know you're straight, absolutely straight, and we both have her interests at heart.'

Suddenly I couldn't bear his boyishness any more. I said, 'I don't care that for her interests. You can have her interests. I only want her body. I want her in bed with me. I'd rather ruin her and sleep with her than, than . . . look after her damned interests.'

He said, 'Oh,' in a weak voice, in the dark.

I went on, 'If it's only her interests you care about, for God's sake leave Phuong alone. Like any other woman she'd rather have a good . . .' The crash of a mortar saved Boston ears from the Anglo-Saxon word.

But there was a quality of the implacable in Pyle. He had determined I was behaving well and I had to behave well. He said, 'I know what you are suffering, Thomas.'

'I'm not suffering.'

'Oh yes, you are. I know what I'd suffer if I had to give up Phuong.'

'But I haven't given her up.'

'I'm pretty physical too, Thomas, but I'd give up all hope of that if I could see Phuong happy.'

59

'She is happy.'

'She can't be – not in her situation. She needs children.'

'Do you really believe all that nonsense her sister . . .'

'A sister sometimes knows better . . .'

'She was just trying to sell the notion to you, Pyle, because she thinks you have more money. And, my God, she has sold it all right.'

'I've only got my salary.'

'Well, you've got a favourable rate of exchange anyway.'

'Don't be bitter, Thomas. These things happen. I wish it had happened to anybody else but you. Are those our mortars?'

'Yes, "our" mortars. You talk as though she was leaving me, Pyle.'

'Of course,' he said without conviction, 'she may choose to stay with you.'

'What would you do then?'

'I'd apply for a transfer.'

'Why don't you just go away, Pyle, without causing trouble?'

'It wouldn't be fair to her, Thomas,' he said quite seriously. I never knew a man who had better motives for all the trouble he caused. He added, 'I don't think you quite understand Phuong.'

And waking that morning months later with Phuong beside me, I thought, 'And did you understand her either? Could you have anticipated this situation? Phuong so happily asleep beside me and you dead?' Time has its revenges, but revenges seem so often sour. Wouldn't we all do better not trying to understand, accepting the fact that no human being will ever understand another, not a wife a husband, a lover a mistress, nor a parent a child? Perhaps that's why men have invented God – a being capable of understanding. Perhaps if I wanted to be understood or to understand I would bamboozle myself into belief, but I am a reporter; God exists only for leader-writers.

'Are you sure there's anything much to understand?' I asked Pyle. 'Oh, for God's sake, let's have a whisky. It's too noisy to argue.'

'It's a little early,' Pyle said.

'It's damned late.'

I poured out two glasses and Pyle raised his and stared through the whisky at the light of the candle. His hand shook whenever a shell burst, and yet he had made that senseless trip from Nam Dinh.

Pyle said, 'It's a strange thing that neither of us can say "Good luck".' So we drank saying nothing.

Chapter 5

1

I HAD thought I would be only one week away from Saigon, but it was nearly three weeks before I returned. In the first place it proved more difficult to get out of the Phat Diem area than it had been to get in. The road was cut between Nam Dinh and Hanoi and aerial transport could not be spared for one reporter who shouldn't have been there anyway. Then when I reached Hanoi the correspondents had been flown up for briefing on the latest victory and the plane that took them back had no seat left for me. Pyle got away from Phat Diem the morning he arrived: he had fulfilled his mission – to speak to me about Phuong, and there was nothing to keep him. I left him asleep when the mortar-fire stopped at five-thirty and when I returned from a cup of coffee and some biscuits in the mess he wasn't there. I assumed that he had gone for a stroll – after punting all the way down the river from Nam Dinh a few snipers would not have worried him; he was as incapable of imagining pain or danger to himself as he was incapable of conceiving the pain he might cause others. On one occasion – but that was months later – I lost control and thrust his foot into it, into the pain I mean, and I remember how he turned away and looked at his stained shoe in perplexity and said, 'I must get a shine before I see the Minister.' I knew then he was already forming his phrases in the style he had learnt from York Harding. Yet he was sincere in his way: it was coincidence that the sacrifices were all paid by others, until that final night under the bridge to Dakow.

It was only when I returned to Saigon that I learnt how Pyle, while I drank my coffee, had persuaded a young naval officer to take him on a landing-craft which after a routine patrol dropped him surreptitiously at Nam Dinh. Luck was with him and he got back to Hanoi with his trachoma team twenty-four hours before the road was officially regarded as cut. When I reached Hanoi he had already left for the south, leaving me a note with the barman at the Press Camp.

'Dear Thomas,' he wrote, 'I can't begin to tell you how swell you were the other night. I can tell you my heart was in my mouth when I walked into that room to find you.' (Where had it been on the long boat-ride down the river?) 'There are not many men who would have taken the whole thing so calmly. You were great, and I don't feel half as mean as I did, now that I've told you.' (Was he the only one that mattered? I wondered angrily, and yet I knew that he didn't intend it that way. To him the whole affair would be happier as soon as he didn't feel mean – I would be happier, Phuong would be happier, the whole world would be happier, even the Economic Attaché and the Minister. Spring had come to Indo-China now that Pyle was mean no longer.) 'I waited for you here for twenty-four hours, but I shan't get back to Saigon for a week if I don't leave today, and my real work is in the south. I've told the boys who are running the trachoma teams to look you up – you'll like them. They are great boys and doing a man-size job. Don't worry in any way that I'm returning to Saigon ahead of you. I promise you I won't see Phuong until you return. I don't want you to feel later that I've been unfair in any way. Cordially yours, Alden.'

Again that calm assumption that 'later' it would be I who would lose Phuong. Is confidence based on a rate of exchange? We used to speak of sterling qualities. Have we got to talk now about a dollar love? A dollar love, of course, would include marriage and Junior and Mother's Day, even though later it might include Reno or the Virgin Islands or wherever they go nowadays for their divorces. A dollar love had good intentions, a clear conscience, and to Hell with everybody. But my love had no intentions: it knew the future. All one could do was try to make the future less hard, to break the future gently when it came, and even opium had its value there. But I never foresaw that the first future I would have to break to Phuong would be the death of Pyle.

I went – for I had nothing better to do – to the Press Conference. Granger, of course, was there. A young and too

63

beautiful French colonel presided. He spoke in French and a junior officer translated. The French correspondents sat together like a rival football-team. I found it hard to keep my mind on what the colonel was saying: all the time it wandered back to Phuong and the one thought – suppose Pyle is right and I lose her: where does one go from here?

The interpreter said, 'The colonel tells you that the enemy has suffered a sharp defeat and severe losses – the equivalent of one complete battalion. The last detachments are now making their way back across the Red River on improvised rafts. They are shelled all the time by the Air Force.' The colonel ran his hand through his elegant yellow hair and, flourishing his pointer, danced his way down the long maps on the wall. An American correspondent asked, 'What are the French losses?'

The colonel knew perfectly well the meaning of the question – it was usually put at this stage of the conference, but he paused, pointer raised with a kind smile like a popular schoolmaster, until it was interpreted. Then he answered with patient ambiguity.

'The colonel says our losses have not been heavy. The exact number is not yet known.'

This was always the signal for trouble. You would have thought that sooner or later the colonel would have found a formula for dealing with his refractory class, or that the headmaster would have appointed a member of his staff more efficient at keeping order.

'Is the colonel seriously telling us,' Granger said, 'that he's had time to count the enemy dead and not his own?'

Patiently the colonel wove his web of evasion, which he knew perfectly well would be destroyed again by another question. The French correspondents sat gloomily silent. If the American correspondents stung the colonel into an admission they would be quick to seize it, but they would not join in baiting their countryman.

'The colonel says the enemy forces are being over-run. It is possible to count the dead behind the firing-line, but while the battle is still in progress you cannot expect figures from the advancing French units.'

'It's not what *we* expect,' Granger said, 'it's what the *Etat Major* knows or not. Are you seriously telling us that platoons do not report their casualties as they happen by walkie-talkie?'

The colonel's temper was beginning to fray. If only, I thought, he had called our bluff from the start and told us firmly that he knew the figures but wouldn't say. After all it was their war, not ours. We had no God-given right to information. We didn't have to fight Left-Wing deputies in Paris as well as the troops of Ho Chi Minh between the Red and the Black Rivers. We were not dying.

The colonel suddenly snapped out the information that French casualties had been in a proportion of one to three, then turned his back on us, to stare furiously at his map. These were his men who were dead, his fellow officers, belonging to the same class at St Cyr – not numerals as they were to Granger. Granger said, 'Now we are getting somewhere,' and stared round with oafish triumph at his fellows; the French with heads bent made their sombre notes.

'That's more than can be said in Korea,' I said with deliberate misunderstanding, but I had only given Granger a new line.

'Ask the colonel,' he said, 'what the French are going to do next? He says the enemy's on the run across the Black River . . .'

'Red River,' the interpreter corrected him.

'I don't care what the colour of the river is. What we want to know is what the French are going to do now.'

'The enemy are in flight.'

'What happens when they get to the other side? What are you going to do then? Are you just going to sit down on the other bank and say that's over?' The French officers listened with gloomy patience to Granger's bullying voice. Even humility is required today of the soldier. 'Are you going to drop them Christmas cards?'

The captain interpreted with care, even to the phrase, '*cartes de Noël*'. The colonel gave us a wintry smile. 'Not Christmas cards,' he said.

I think the colonel's youth and beauty particularly irritated Granger. The colonel wasn't – at least not by Granger's interpretation – a man's man. He said, 'You aren't dropping much else.'

The colonel spoke suddenly in English, good English. He said, 'If the supplies promised by the Americans had arrived, we should have more to drop.' He was really in spite of his elegance a simple man. He believed that a newspaper correspondent cared for his country's honour more than for news. Granger said sharply (he was efficient: he kept dates well in his head), 'You mean that none of the supplies promised for the beginning of September have arrived?'

'No.'

Granger had got his news: he began to write.

'I am sorry,' the colonel said, 'that is not for printing: that is for background.'

'But colonel,' Granger protested, 'that's news. We can help you there.'

'No, it is a matter for the diplomats.'

'What harm can it do?'

The French correspondents were at a loss: they could speak very little English. The colonel had broken the rules They muttered angrily together.

'I am no judge,' the colonel said. 'Perhaps the American newspapers would say, "Oh, the French are always complaining, always begging." And in Paris the Communists would accuse, "The French are spilling their blood for America and America will not even send a second-hand helicopter." It does no good. At the end of it we should still have no helicopters, and the enemy would still be there, fifty miles from Hanoi.'

'At least I can print that, can't I, that you need helicopters bad?'

'You can say,' the colonel said, 'that six months ago we had three helicopters and now we have one. One,' he repeated with a kind of amazed bitterness. 'You can say that if a man is wounded in this fighting, not seriously wounded, just wounded, he knows that he is probably a dead man. Twelve hours, twenty-four hours perhaps, on a stretcher to the ambulance, then bad tracks, a breakdown, perhaps an ambush gangrene. It is better to be killed outright.' The French cor respondents leant forward, trying to understand. 'You can write that,' he said, looking all the more venomous for his physical beauty. '*Interprètez*,' he ordered, and walked out of the room leaving the captain the unfamiliar task of translating from English into French.

'Got him on the raw,' said Granger with satisfaction, and he went into a corner by the bar to write his telegram. Mine didn't take long: there was nothing I could write from Phat Diem that the censors would pass. If the story had seemed good enough I could have flown to Hong Kong and sent it from there, but was any news good enough to risk expulsion? I doubted it. Expulsion meant the end of a whole life, it meant the victory of Pyle, and there, when I returned to my hotel, waiting in my pigeon-hole, was in fact his victory, the end of the affair – a congratulatory telegram of promotion. Dante never thought up that turn of the screw for his condemned lovers. Paolo was never promoted to Purgatory.

I went upstairs to my bare room and the dripping cold-water tap (there was no hot water in Hanoi) and sat on the edge of my bed with the bundle of the mosquito-net like a swollen cloud overhead. I was to be the new foreign editor, arriving every afternoon at half past three, at that grim Victorian building near Blackfriars station with a plaque of Lord Salisbury by the lift. They had sent the good news on from Saigon, and I wondered whether it had already reached Phuong's ears. I was to be a reporter no longer: I was to have opinions, and in return for that empty privilege I was deprived of my last hope in the contest with Pyle. I had experience to match his virginity, age was as good a card to play in the sexual game as youth, but now I hadn't even the limited future of twelve more months to offer, and a future was trumps. I envied the most homesick officer condemned to the chance of death. I would have liked to weep, but the ducts were as dry as the hot-water pipes. Oh, they could have home – I only wanted my room in the rue Catinat.

It was cold after dark in Hanoi and the lights were lower than those of Saigon, more suited to the darker clothes of the women and the fact of war. I walked up the rue Gambetta to the Pax Bar – I didn't want to drink in the Metropole with the senior French officers, their wives and their girls, and as I reached the bar I was aware of the distant drumming of the guns out towards Hoa Binh. In the day they were drowned in traffic-noises, but everything was quiet now except for the tring of bicycle-bells where the trishaw drivers plied for hire. Pietri sat in his usual place. He had an odd elongated skull which sat on his shoulders like a pear on a dish; he was a Sureté officer and was married to a pretty Tonkinese who owned the Pax Bar. He was another man who had no particular desire to go home. He was a Corsican, but he preferred Marseilles, and to Marseilles he preferred any day his seat on the pavement in the rue Gambetta. I wondered whether he already knew the contents of my telegram.

'*Quatre Cent Vingt-et-un?*' he asked.

'Why not?'

We began to throw and it seemed impossible to me that I could ever have a life again, away from the rue Gambetta and the rue Catinat, the flat taste of vermouth cassis, the homely click of dice, and the gunfire travelling like a clock-hand around the horizon.

I said, 'I'm going back.'

'Home?' Pietri asked, throwing a four-to-one.

'No. England.'

PART TWO

Chapter 1

PYLE had invited himself for what he called a drink, but I knew very well he didn't really drink. After the passage of weeks that fantastic meeting in Phat Diem seemed hardly believable: even the details of the conversation were less clear. They were like the missing letters on a Roman tomb and I the archaeologist filling in the gaps according to the bias of my scholarship. It even occurred to me that he had been pulling my leg, and that the conversation had been an elaborate and humorous disguise for his real purpose, for it was already the gossip of Saigon that he was engaged in one of those services so ineptly called secret. Perhaps he was arranging American arms for a Third Force – the Bishop's brass band, all that was left of his young scared unpaid levies. The telegram that awaited me in Hanoi I kept in my pocket. There was no point in telling Phuong, for that would be to poison the few months we had left with tears and quarrels. I wouldn't even go for my exit-permit till the last moment in case she had a relation in the immigration-office.

I told her, 'Pyle's coming at six.'

'I will go and see my sister,' she said.

'I expect he'd like to see you.'

'He does not like me or my family. When you were away he did not come once to my sister, although she had invited him. She was very hurt.'

'You needn't go out.'

'If he wanted to see me, he would have asked us to the Majestic. He wants to talk to you privately – about business.'

'What is his business?'

'People say he imports a great many things.'

'What things?'

'Drugs, medicines . . .'

'Those are for the trachoma teams in the north.'

'Perhaps. The Customs must not open them. They are diplomatic parcels. But once there was a mistake – the man was discharged. The First Secretary threatened to stop all imports.'

'What was in the case?'

'Plastic.'

'You don't mean bombs?'

'No. Just plastic.'

When Phuong had gone, I wrote home. A man from Reuter's was leaving for Hong Kong in a few days and he could mail my letter from there. I knew my appeal was hopeless, but I was not going to reproach myself later for not taking every possible measure. I wrote to the Managing Editor that this was the wrong moment to change their correspondent. General de Lattre was dying in Paris: the French were about to withdraw altogether from Hoa Binh: the north had never been in greater danger. I wasn't suitable, I told him, for a foreign editor – I was a reporter, I had no real opinions about anything. On the last page I even appealed to him on personal grounds, although it was unlikely that any human sympathy could survive under the strip-light, among the green eye-shades and the stereotyped phrases – 'the good of the paper', 'the situation demands . . .'

I wrote: 'For private reasons I am very unhappy at being moved from Vietnam. I don't think I can do my best work in England, where there will be not only financial but family strains. Indeed, if I could afford it I would resign rather than return to the U.K. I only mention this as showing the strength of my objection. I don't think you have found me a bad correspondent, and this is the first favour I have ever asked of you.' Then I looked over my article on the battle of Phat Diem, so that I could send it out to be posted under a Hong Kong dateline. The French would not seriously object now – the siege had been raised: a defeat could be played as a victory. Then I tore up the last page of my letter to the editor. It was no use – the 'private reasons' would become only the subject of sly jokes. Every correspondent, it was assumed, had his local girl. The editor would joke to the night-editor, who would take the envious thought back to his semi-detached villa in Streatham and climb into bed with it beside the faith-

72

ful wife he had carried with him years back from Glasgow. I could see so well the kind of house that has no mercy – a broken tricycle stood in the hall and somebody had broken his favourite pipe; and there was a child's shirt in the living-room waiting for a button to be sewn on. 'Private reasons': drinking in the Press Club I wouldn't want to be reminded by their jokes of Phuong.

There was a knock on the door. I opened it to Pyle and his black dog walked in ahead of him. Pyle looked over my shoulder and found the room empty. 'I'm alone,' I said, 'Phuong is with her sister.' He blushed. I noticed that he was wearing a Hawaii shirt, even though it was comparatively restrained in colour and design. I was surprised: had he been accused of un-American activities? He said, 'I hope I haven't interrupted . . .'

'Of course not. Have a drink?'

'Thanks. Beer?'

'Sorry. We haven't a frig – we send out for ice. What about a Scotch?'

'A small one, if you don't mind. I'm not very keen on hard liquor.'

'On the rocks?'

'Plenty of soda – if you aren't short.'

I said, 'I haven't seen you since Phat Diem.'

'You got my note, Thomas?'

When he used my Christian name, it was like a declaration that he hadn't been humorous, that he hadn't been covering up, that he was here to get Phuong. I noticed that his crew-cut had recently been trimmed; was even the Hawaii shirt serving the function of male plumage?

'I got your note,' I said. 'I suppose I ought to knock you down.'

'Of course,' he said, 'you've every right, Thomas. But I boxed at college – and I'm so much younger.'

'No, it wouldn't be a good move for me, would it?'

'You know, Thomas (I'm sure you feel the same), I don't like discussing Phuong behind her back. I thought she would be here.'

73

'Well, what shall we discuss – plastic?' I hadn't meant to surprise him.

He said, 'You know about that?'

'Phuong told me.'

'How could she . . . ?'

'You can be sure it's all over the town. What's so important about it? Are you going into the toy business?'

'We don't like the details of our aid to get around. You know what Congress is like – and then one has visiting Senators. We had a lot of trouble about our trachoma teams because they were using one drug instead of another.'

'I still don't understand the plastic.'

His black dog sat on the floor taking up too much room, panting; its tongue looked like a burnt pancake. Pyle said vaguely, 'Oh, you know, we want to get some of these local industries on their feet, and we have to be careful of the French. They want everything bought in France.'

'I don't blame them. A war needs money.'

'Do you like dogs?'

'No.'

'I thought the British were great dog-lovers.'

'We think Americans love dollars, but there must be exceptions.'

'I don't know how I'd get along without Duke. You know sometimes I feel so darned lonely . . .'

'You've got a great many companions in your branch.'

'The first dog I ever had was called Prince. I called him after the Black Prince. You know, the fellow who . . .'

'Massacred all the women and children in Limoges.'

'I don't remember that.'

'The history books gloss it over.'

I was to see many times that look of pain and disappointment touch his eyes and mouth when reality didn't match the romantic ideas he cherished, or when someone he loved or admired dropped below the impossible standard he had set. Once, I remember, I caught York Harding out in a gross error of fact, and I had to comfort him: 'It's human to make mistakes.' He had laughed nervously and said, 'You must think me a fool, but – well, I almost thought him infallible.'

He added, 'My father took to him a lot the only time they met, and my father's darned difficult to please.'

The big black dog called Duke, having panted long enough to establish a kind of right to the air, began to poke about the room. 'Could you ask your dog to be still?' I said.

'Oh, I'm so sorry. Duke. Duke. Sit down, Duke.' Duke sat down and began noisily to lick his private parts. I filled our glasses and managed in passing to disturb Duke's toilet. The quiet lasted a very short time; he began to scratch himself.

'Duke's awfully intelligent,' said Pyle.

'What happened to Prince?'

'We were down on the farm in Connecticut and he got run over.'

'Were you upset?'

'Oh, I minded a lot. He meant a great deal to me, but one has to be sensible. Nothing could bring him back.'

'And if you lose Phuong, will you be sensible?'

'Oh yes, I hope so. And you?'

'I doubt it. I might even run amok. Have you thought about that, Pyle?'

'I wish you'd call me Alden, Thomas.'

'I'd rather not. Pyle has got − associations. Have you thought about it?'

'Of course I haven't. You're the straightest guy I've ever known. When I remember how you behaved when I barged in . . .'

'I remember thinking before I went to sleep how convenient it would be if there were an attack and you were killed. A hero's death. For Democracy.'

'Don't laugh at me, Thomas.' He shifted his long limbs uneasily. 'I must seem a bit dumb to you, but I know when you're kidding.'

'I'm not.'

'I know if you come clean you want what's best for her.'

It was then I heard Phuong's step. I had hoped against hope that he would have gone before she returned. He heard it too and recognized it. He said, 'There she is,' although he had had only one evening to learn her footfall. Even the dog got up and stood by the door, which I had left open for coolness, almost as though he accepted her as one of Pyle's family. I was an intruder.

Phuong said, 'My sister was not in,' and looked guardedly at Pyle.

I wondered whether she were telling the truth or whether her sister had ordered her to hurry back.

'You remember Monsieur Pyle?' I said.

'*Enchantée.*' She was on her best behaviour.

'I'm so pleased to see you again,' he said, blushing.

'*Comment?*'

'Her English is not very good,' I said.

'I'm afraid my French is awful. I'm taking lessons though. And I can understand – if Phuong will speak slowly.'

'I'll act as interpreter,' I said. 'The local accent takes some getting used to. Now what do you want to say? Sit down, Phuong. Monsieur Pyle has come specially to see you. Are you sure,' I added to Pyle, 'that you wouldn't like me to leave you two alone?'

'I want you to hear everything I have to say. It wouldn't be fair otherwise.'

'Well, fire away.'

He said solemnly, as though this part he had learned by heart, that he had a great love and respect for Phuong. He had felt it ever since the night he had danced with her. I was reminded a little of a butler showing a party of tourists over a 'great house'. The great house was his heart, and of the private apartments where the family lived we were given only a rapid and surreptitious glimpse. I translated for him with meticulous care – it sounded worse that way, and Phuong sat quiet with her hands in her lap as though she were listening to a movie.

'Has she understood that?' he asked.

'As far as I can tell. You don't want me to add a little fire to it, do you?'

'Oh no,' he said, 'just translate. I don't want to sway her emotionally.'

'I see.'

'Tell her I want to marry her.'

I told her.

'What was that she said?'

'She asked me if you were serious. I told her you were the serious type.'

'I suppose this is an odd situation,' he said. 'Me asking you to translate.'

'Rather odd.'

'And yet it seems so natural. After all you are my best friend.'

'It's kind of you to say so.'

'There's nobody I'd go to in trouble sooner than you,' he said.

'And I suppose being in love with my girl is a kind of trouble?'

'Of course. I wish it was anybody but you, Thomas.'

'Well, what do I say to her next. That you can't live without her?'

'No, that's too emotional. It's not quite true either. I'd have to go away, of course, but one gets over everything.'

'While you are thinking what to say, do you mind if I put in a word for myself?'

'No, of course not, it's only fair, Thomas.'

'Well, Phuong,' I said, 'are you going to leave me for him? He'll marry you. I can't. You know why.'

'Are you going away?' she asked and I thought of the editor's letter in my pocket.

'No.'

'Never?'

'How can one promise that? He can't either. Marriages break. Often they break quicker than an affair like ours.'

'I do not want to go,' she said, but the sentence was not comforting; it contained an unexpressed 'but'.

Pyle said, 'I think I ought to put all my cards on the table. I'm not rich. But when my father dies I'll have about fifty thousand dollars. I'm in good health – I've got a medical certificate only two months old, and I can let her know my blood-group.'

'I don't know how to translate that. What's it for?'

'Well, to make certain we can have children together.'

'Is that how you make love in America – figures of income and blood-group?'

'I don't know, I've never done it before. Maybe at home my mother would talk to her mother.'

'About your blood-group?'

'Don't laugh at me, Thomas. I expect I'm old-fashioned. You know I'm a little lost in this situation.'

'So am I. Don't you think we might call it off and dice for her?'

'Now you are pretending to be tough, Thomas. I know you love her in your way as much as I do.'

'Well, go on, Pyle.'

'Tell her I don't expect her to love me right away. That will come in time, but tell her what I offer is security and respect. That doesn't sound very exciting, but perhaps it's better than passion.'

'She can always get passion,' I said, 'with your chauffeur when you are away at the office.'

Pyle blushed. He got awkwardly to his feet and said, 'That's a dirty crack. I won't have her insulted. You've no right ...'

'She's not your wife yet.'

'What can you offer her?' he asked with anger. 'A couple of hundred dollars when you leave for England, or will you pass her on with the furniture?'

'The furniture isn't mine.'

'She's not either. Phuong, will you marry me?'

'What about the blood-group?' I said. 'And a health certificate. You'll need hers, surely? Maybe you ought to have mine too. And her horoscope – no, that's an Indian custom.'

'Will you marry me?'

'Say it in French,' I said, 'I'm damned if I'll interpret for you any more.'

I got to my feet and the dog growled. It made me furious. 'Tell your damned Duke to be quiet. This is my home, not his.'

'Will you marry me?' he repeated. I took a step towards Phuong and the dog growled again.

I said to Phuong, 'Tell him to go away and take his dog with him.'

'Come away with me now,' Pyle said. '*Avec moi.*'

'No,' Phuong said, 'no.' Suddenly all the anger in both of us vanished; it was a problem as simple as that: it could be solved with a word of two letters. I felt an enormous relief; Pyle stood there with his mouth a little open and an expression of bewilderment on his face. He said, 'She said no.'

'She knows that much English.' I wanted to laugh now: what fools we had both made of each other. I said, 'Sit down and have another Scotch, Pyle.'

'I think I ought to go.'

'One for the road.'

'Mustn't drink all your whisky,' he muttered.

'I get all I want through the Legation.' I moved towards the table and the dog bared its teeth.

Pyle said furiously, 'Down, Duke. Behave yourself.' He wiped the sweat off his forehead. 'I'm awfully sorry, Thomas, if I said anything I shouldn't. I don't know what came over me.' He took the glass and said wistfully, 'The best man wins. Only please don't leave her, Thomas.'

Of course I shan't leave her,' I said.

Phuong said to me, 'Would he like to smoke a pipe?'

'Would you like to smoke a pipe?'

'No, thank you. I don't touch opium and we have strict rules in the service. I'll just drink this up and be off. I'm sorry about Duke. He's very quiet as a rule.'

'Stay to supper.'

'I think, if you don't mind, I'd rather be alone.' He gave an uncertain grin. 'I suppose people would say we'd both behaved rather strangely. I wish you could marry her, Thomas.'

'Do you really?'

'Yes. Ever since I saw that place – you know, that house near the Chalet – I've been so afraid.'

He drank his unaccustomed whisky quickly, not looking at Phuong, and when he said good-bye he didn't touch her hand, but gave an awkward little bobbing bow. I noticed how her eyes followed him to the door and as I passed the mirror I saw myself: the top button of my trousers undone, the beginning of a paunch. Outside he said, 'I promise not to see her, Thomas. You won't let this come between us, will you? I'll get a transfer when I finish my tour.'

'When's that?'

'About two years.'

I went back to the room and I thought. 'What's the good? I might as well have told them both that I was going.' He had only to carry his bleeding heart for a few weeks as a decoration ... My lie would even ease his conscience.

'Shall I make you a pipe?' Phuong asked.

'Yes, in a moment. I just want to write a letter.'

It was the second letter of the day, but I tore none of this up, though I had as little hope of a response. I wrote: 'Dear Helen, I am coming back to England next April to take the job of foreign editor. You can imagine I am not very happy about it. England is to me the scene of my failure. I had intended our marriage to last quite as much as if I had shared your Christian beliefs. To this day I'm not certain what went wrong (I know we both tried), but I think it was my temper. I know how cruel and bad my temper can be. Now I think it's a little better – the East has done that for me – not sweeter, but quieter. Perhaps it's simply that I'm five years older – at the end of life when five years becomes a high proportion of what's left. You have been very generous to me, and you have never reproached me once since our separation. Would you be even more generous? I know that before we married you warned me there could never be a divorce. I accepted the risk and I've nothing to complain of. At the same time I'm asking for one now.'

Phuong called out to me from the bed that she had the tray ready.

'A moment,' I said.

'I could wrap this up,' I wrote, 'and make it sound more honourable and more dignified by pretending it was for someone else's sake. But it isn't, and we always used to tell each other the truth. It's for my sake and only mine. I love someone very much, we have lived together for more than two years, she has been very loyal to me, but I know I'm not essential to her. If I leave her, she'll be a little unhappy I think, but there won't be any tragedy. She'll marry someone else and have a family. It's stupid of me to tell you this. I'm putting a reply into your mouth. But because I've been truthful so far, perhaps you'll believe me when I tell you that to lose her will be, for me, the beginning of death. I'm not asking you to be "reasonable" (reason is all on your side) or to be merciful. It's too big a word for my situation and anyway I don't particularly deserve mercy. I suppose what I'm really. asking you is to behave, all of a sudden, irrationally, out of character. I want you to feel' (I hesitated over the word and then I didn't get it right) 'affection and to act before you have time to think. I know that's easier done over a telephone than over eight thousand miles. If only you'd just cable me "I agree"!'

When I had finished I felt as though I had run a long way and strained unconditioned muscles. I lay down on the bed while Phuong made my pipe. I said, 'He's young.'

'Who?'

'Pyle.'

'That's not so important.'

'I would marry you if I could, Phuong.'

'I think so, but my sister does not believe it.'

'I have just written to my wife and I have asked her to divorce me. I have never tried before. There is always a chance.'

'A big chance?'

'No, but a small one.'

'Don't worry. Smoke.'

I drew in the smoke and she began to prepare my second pipe. I asked her again, 'Was your sister really not at home, Phuong?'

'I told you – she was out.' It was absurd to subject her to this passion for truth, an Occidental passion, like the passion for alcohol. Because of the whisky I had drunk with Pyle, the effect of the opium was lessened. I said, 'I lied to you, Phuong. I have been ordered home.'

She put the pipe down. 'But you won't go?'

'If I refused, what would we live on?'

'I could come with you. I would like to see London.'

'It would be very uncomfortable for you if we were not married.'

'But perhaps your wife will divorce you.'

'Perhaps.'

'I will come with you anyway,' she said. She meant it, but I could see in her eyes the long train of thoughts begin, as she lifted the pipe again and began to warm the pellet of opium. She said, 'Are there skyscrapers in London?' and I loved her for the innocence of her question. She might lie from politeness, from fear, even for profit, but she would never have the cunning to keep her lie concealed.

'No,' I said, 'you have to go to America for them.'

She gave me a quick look over the needle and registered her mistake. Then as she kneaded the opium she began to talk at random of what clothes she would wear in London, where we should live, of the tube-trains she had read about in a novel, and the double-decker buses: would we fly or go by sea? 'And the Statue of Liberty . . .' she said.

'No, Phuong, that's American too.'

Chapter 2

AT least once a year the Caodaists hold a festival at the Holy
See in Tanyin, which lies eighty kilometres to the north-west
of Saigon, to celebrate such and such a year of Liberation, or
of Conquest, or even a Buddhist, Confucian or Christian
festival. Caodaism was always the favourite chapter of my
briefing to visitors. Caodaism, the invention of a Cochin civil
servant, was a synthesis of the three religions. The Holy See
was at Tanyin. A Pope and female cardinals. Prophecy by
planchette. Saint Victor Hugo. Christ and Buddha looking
down from the roof of the Cathedral on a Walt Disney fan-
tasia of the East, dragons and snakes in technicolour. New-
comers were always delighted with the description. How
could one explain the dreariness of the whole business: the
private army of twenty-five thousand men, armed with mortars
made out of the exhaust-pipes of old cars, allies of the French
who turned neutral at the moment of danger? To these
celebrations, which helped to keep the peasants quiet, the Pope
invited members of the Government (who would turn up if
the Caodaists at the moment held office), the Diplomatic
Corps (who would send a few second secretaries with their
wives or girls) and the French Commander-in-Chief, who
would detail a two-star general from an office job to represent
him.

Along the route to Tanyin flowed a fast stream of staff and
C.D. cars, and on the more exposed sections of the road
Foreign Legionaries threw out cover across the rice-fields. It
was always a day of some anxiety for the French High Command and perhaps a certain hope for the Caodaists, for what
could more painlessly emphasize their own loyalty than to
have a few important guests shot outside their territory?

Every kilometre a small mud watch tower stood up above
the flat fields like an exclamation-mark, and every ten kilometres there was a larger fort manned by a platoon of Legionaries, Moroccans or Senegalese. Like the traffic into New York

the cars kept one pace – and as with the traffic into New York you had a sense of controlled impatience, watching the next car ahead and in the mirror the car behind. Everybody wanted to reach Tanyin, see the show and get back as quickly as possible: curfew was at seven.

One passed out of the French-controlled rice-fields into the rice-fields of the Hoa-Haos and thence into the rice-fields of the Caodaists, who were usually at war with the Hoa-Haos: only the flags changed on the watch towers. Small naked boys sat on the buffaloes which waded genital-deep among the irrigated fields; where the gold harvest was ready the peasants in their hats like limpets winnowed the rice against little curved shelters of plaited bamboo. The cars drove rapidly by, belonging to another world.

Now the churches of the Caodaists would catch the attention of strangers in every village; pale blue and pink plasterwork and a big eye of God over the door. Flags increased: troops of peasants made their way along the road: we were approaching the Holy See. In the distance the sacred mountain stood like a green bowler hat above Tanyin – that was where General Thé held out, the dissident Chief of Staff who had recently declared his intention of fighting both the French and the Vietminh. The Caodaists made no attempt to capture him, although he had kidnapped a cardinal, but it was rumoured that he had done it with the Pope's connivance.

It always seemed hotter in Tanyin than anywhere else in the Southern Delta; perhaps it was the absence of water, perhaps it was the sense of interminable ceremonies which made one sweat vicariously, sweat for the troops standing to attention through the long speeches in a language they didn't understand, sweat for the Pope in his heavy chinoiserie robes. Only the female cardinals in their white silk trousers chatting to the priests in sun-helmets gave an impression of coolness under the glare; you couldn't believe it would ever be seven o'clock and cocktail-time on the roof of the Majestic, with a wind from Saigon river.

After the parade I interviewed the Pope's deputy. I didn't expect to get anything out of him and I was right: it was a convention on both sides. I asked him about General Thé.

'A rash man,' he said and dismissed the subject. He began his set speech, forgetting that I had heard it two years before – it reminded me of my own gramophone records for new-comers. Caodaism was a religious synthesis ... the best of all religions ... missionaries had been despatched to Los Angeles ... the secrets of the Great Pyramid ... He wore a long white soutane and he chain-smoked. There was something cunning and corrupt about him: the word 'love' occurred often. I was certain he knew that all of us were there to laugh at his movement; our air of respect was as corrupt as his phoney hierarchy, but we were less cunning. Our hypocrisy gained us nothing – not even a reliable ally, while theirs had procured arms, supplies, even cash down.

'Thank you, your Eminence.' I got up to go. He came with me to the door, scattering cigarette-ash.

'God's blessing on your work,' he said unctuously. 'Remember God loves the truth.'

'Which truth?' I asked.

'In the Caodaist faith all truths are reconciled and truth is love.'

He had a large ring on his finger and, when he held out his hand I really think he expected me to kiss it, but I am not a diplomat.

Under the bleak vertical sunlight I saw Pyle; he was trying in vain to make his Buick start. Somehow, during the last two weeks, at the bar of the Continental, in the only good book-shop in the rue Catinat, I had continually run into Pyle. The friendship which he had imposed from the beginning he now emphasized more than ever. His sad eyes would inquire with fervour after Phuong, while his lips expressed with even more fervour the strength of his affection and of his admiration – God save the mark – for me.

A Caodaist commandant stood beside the car talking rapidly. He stopped when I came up. I recognized him – he had been one of Thé's assistants before Thé took to the hills.

'Hullo, commandant,' I said, 'how's the General?'

'Which general?' he asked with a shy grin.

'Surely in the Caodaist faith,' I said, 'all generals are reconciled.'

'I can't make this car move, Thomas,' Pyle said.

'I will get a mechanic,' the commandant said, and left us.

'I interrupted you.'

'Oh, it was nothing,' Pyle said. 'He wanted to know how much a Buick cost. These people are so friendly when you treat them right. The French don't seem to know how to handle them.'

'The French don't trust them.'

Pyle said solemnly, 'A man becomes trustworthy when you trust him.' It sounded like a Caodaist maxim. I began to feel the air of Tanyin was too ethical for me to breathe.

'Have a drink,' Pyle said.

'There's nothing I'd like better.'

'I brought a thermos of lime-juice with me.' He leant over and busied himself with a basket in the back.

'Any gin?'

'No, I'm awfully sorry. You know,' he said encouragingly, 'lime-juice is very good for you in this climate. It contains – I'm not sure which vitamins.' He held out a cup to me and I drank.

'Anyway, it's wet,' I said.

'Like a sandwich? They're really awfully good. A new sandwich-spread called Vit-Health. My mother sent it from the States.'

'No, thanks, I'm not hungry.'

'It tastes rather like Russian salad – only sort of drier.'

'I don't think I will.'

'You don't mind if I do?'

'No, no, of course not.'

He took a large mouthful and it crunched and crackled. In the distance Buddha in white and pink stone rode away from his ancestral home and his valet – another statue – pursued him running. The female cardinals were drifting back to their house and the Eye of God watched us from above the Cathedral door.

'You know they are serving lunch here?' I said.

'I thought I wouldn't risk it. The meat – you have to be careful in this heat.'

'You are quite safe. They are vegetarian.'

'I suppose it's all right – but I like to know what I'm eating.' He took another munch at his Vit-Health. 'Do you think they have any reliable mechanics?'

'They know enough to turn your exhaust pipe into a mortar. I believe Buicks make the best mortars.'

The commandant returned and, saluting us smartly, said he had sent to the barracks for a mechanic. Pyle offered him a Vit-Health sandwich, which he refused politely. He said with a man-of-the-world air, 'We have so many rules here about food.' (He spoke excellent English.) 'So foolish. But you know what it is in a religious capital. I expect it is the same thing in Rome – or Canterbury,' he added with a neat natty little bow to me. Then he was silent. They were both silent. I had a strong impression that my company was not wanted. I couldn't resist the temptation to tease Pyle – it is, after all, the weapon of weakness and I was weak. I hadn't youth, seriousness, integrity, a future. I said, 'Perhaps after all I'll have a sandwich.'

'Oh, of course,' Pyle said, 'of course.' He paused before turning to the basket in the back.

'No, no,' I said. 'I was only joking. You two want to be alone.'

'Nothing of the kind,' Pyle said. He was one of the most inefficient liars I have ever known – it was an art he had obviously never practised. He explained to the commandant, 'Thomas here's the best friend I have.'

'I know Mr Fowler,' the commandant said.

'I'll see you before I go, Pyle.' And I walked away to the Cathedral. I could get some coolness there.

Saint Victor Hugo in the uniform of the French Academy with the halo round his tricorn hat pointed at some noble sentiment Sun Yat Sen was inscribing on a tablet, and then I was in the nave. There was nowhere to sit except in the Papal chair, round which a plaster cobra coiled, the marble floor glittered like water and there was no glass in the windows. We make a cage for air with holes, I thought, and man makes a cage for his religion in much the same way – with doubts left open to the weather and creeds opening on innumerable interpretations. My wife had found her cage with holes and sometimes I envied her. There is a conflict between sun and air: I lived too much in the sun.

I walked the long empty nave – this was not the Indo-China I loved. The dragons with lion-like heads climbed the pulpit: on the roof Christ exposed his bleeding heart. Buddha sat, as Buddha always sits, with his lap empty. Confucius's beard hung meagrely down like a waterfall in the dry season. This was play-acting: the great globe above the altar was ambition: the basket with the movable lid in which the Pope worked his prophecies was trickery. If this Cathedral had existed for five centuries instead of two decades, would it have gathered a kind of convincingness with the scratches of feet and the erosion of weather? Would somebody who was convincible like my wife find here a faith she couldn't find in human beings? And if I had really wanted faith would I have found it in her Norman church? But I had never desired faith. The job of a reporter is to expose and record. I had never in my career discovered the inexplicable. The Pope worked his prophecies with a pencil in a movable lid and the people believed. In any vision somewhere you could find the planchette. I had no visions or miracles in my repertoire of memory.

I turned my memories over at random like pictures in an album: a fox I had seen by the light of an enemy flare over Orpington stealing along beside a fowl run, out of his russet place in the marginal country: the body of a bayoneted Malay which a Gurkha patrol had brought at the back of a lorry into a mining camp in Pahang, and the Chinese coolies stood by and giggled with nerves, while a brother Malay put a cushion under the dead head: a pigeon on a mantelpiece, poised for flight in a hotel bedroom: my wife's face at a window when I came home to say good-bye for the last time. My thoughts had begun and ended with her. She must have received my letter more than a week ago, and the cable I did not expect had not come. But they say if a jury remains out for long enough there is hope for the prisoner. In another week, if no letter arrived, could I begin to hope? All round me I could hear the cars of the soldiers and the diplomats revving up: the party was over for another year. The stampede back to Saigon was beginning, and curfew called. I went out to look for Pyle.

He was standing in a patch of shade with his commandant, and no one was doing anything to his car. The conversation seemed to be over, whatever it had been about, and they stood silently there, constrained by mutual politeness. I joined them.

'Well,' I said, 'I think I'll be off. You'd better be leaving too if you want to be in before curfew.'

'The mechanic hasn't turned up.'

'He will come soon,' the commandant said. 'He was in the parade.'

'You could spend the night,' I said. 'There's a special Mass – you'll find it quite an experience. It lasts three hours.'

'I ought to get back.'

'You won't get back unless you start now.' I added unwillingly, 'I'll give you a lift if you like and the commandant can have your car sent in to Saigon tomorrow.'

'You need not bother about curfew in Caodaist territory,' the commandant said smugly. 'But beyond . . . Certainly I will have your car sent tomorrow.'

'Exhaust intact,' I said, and he smiled brightly, neatly, efficiently, a military abbreviation of a smile.

2

The procession of cars was well ahead of us by the time we started. I put on speed to try to overtake it, but we had passed out of the Caodaist zone into the zone of the Hoa-Haos with not even a dust cloud ahead of us. The world was flat and empty in the evening.

It was not the kind of country one associates with ambush, but men could conceal themselves neck-deep in the drowned fields within a few yards of the road.

Pyle cleared his throat and it was the signal for an approaching intimacy. 'I hope Phuong's well,' he said.

'I've never known her ill.' One watch tower sank behind, another appeared, like weights on a balance.

'I saw her sister out shopping yesterday.'

'And I suppose she asked you to look in,' I said.

'As a matter of fact she did.'

'She doesn't give up hope easily.'

'Hope?'

'Of marrying you to Phuong.'

'She told me you are going away.'

'These rumours get about.'

Pyle said, 'You'd play straight with me, Thomas, wouldn't you?'

'Straight?'

'I've applied for a transfer,' he said. 'I wouldn't want her to be left without either of us.'

'I thought you were going to see your time out.'

He said without self-pity, 'I found I couldn't stand it.'

'When are you leaving?'

'I don't know. They thought something could be arranged in six months.'

'You can stand six months?'

'I've got to.'

'What reason did you give?'

'I told the Economic Attaché – you met him – Joe – more or less the facts.'

'I suppose he thinks I'm a bastard not to let you walk off with my girl.'

'Oh no, he rather sided with you.'

The car was spluttering and heaving – it had been spluttering for a minute, I think, before I noticed it, for I had been examining Pyle's innocent question: 'Are you playing straight?' It belonged to a psychological world of great simplicity, where you talked of Democracy and Honor without the *u* as it's spelt on old tombstones, and you meant what your father meant by the same words. I said, 'We've run out.'

'Gas?'

'There was plenty. I crammed it full before I started. Those bastards in Tanyin have syphoned it out. I ought to have noticed. It's like them to leave us enough to get out of their zone.'

'What shall we do?'

'We can just make the next watch tower. Let's hope they have a little.'

But we were out of luck. The car reached within thirty yards of the tower and gave up. We walked to the foot of the tower and I called up in French to the guards that we were friends, that we were coming up. I had no wish to be shot by a Vietnamese sentry. There was no reply: nobody looked out. I said to Pyle, 'Have you a gun?'

'I never carry one.'

'Nor do I.'

The last colours of sunset, green and gold like the rice, were dripping over the edge of the flat world: against the grey neutral sky the watch tower looked as black as print. It must be nearly the hour of curfew. I shouted again and nobody answered.

'Do you know how many towers we passed since the last fort?'

'I wasn't noticing.'

'Nor was I.' It was probably at least six kilometres to the next fort – an hour's walk. I called a third time, and silence repeated itself like an answer.

I said, 'It seems to be empty: I'd better climb up and see.' The yellow flag with red stripes faded to orange showed that we were out of the territory of the Hoa-Haos and in the territory of the Vietnamese army.

Pyle said, 'Don't you think if we waited here a car might come?'

'It might, but *they* might come first.'

'Shall I go back and turn on the lights? For a signal.'

'Good God, no. Let it be.' It was dark enough now to stumble, looking for the ladder. Something cracked under foot; I could imagine the sound travelling across the fields of paddy, listened to by whom? Pyle had lost his outline and was a blur at the side of the road. Darkness, when once it fell, fell like a stone. I said, 'Stay there until I call.' I wondered whether the guard would have drawn up his ladder, but there it stood – though an enemy might climb it, it was their only way of escape. I began to mount.

I have read so often of people's thoughts in the moment of
fear: of God, or family, or a woman. I admire their control.
I thought of nothing, not even of the trap-door above me: I
ceased, for those seconds, to exist: I was fear taken neat. At
the top of the ladder I banged my head because fear couldn't
count steps, hear, or see. Then my head came over the earth
floor and nobody shot at me and fear seeped away.

3

A small oil lamp burned on the floor and two men crouched
against the wall, watching me. One had a sten gun and one a
rifle, but they were as scared as I'd been. They looked like
schoolboys, but with the Vietnamese age drops suddenly like
the sun – they are boys and then they are old men. I was glad
that the colour of my skin and the shape of my eyes were a
passport – they wouldn't shoot now even from fear.

I came up out of the floor, talking to reassure them, telling
them that my car was outside, that I had run out of petrol.
Perhaps they had a little I could buy. It didn't seem likely as
I stared around. There was nothing in the little round room
except a box of ammunition for the sten gun, a small wooden
bed, and two packs hanging on a nail. A couple of pans with
the remains of rice and some wooden chopsticks showed they
had been eating without much appetite.

'Just enough to get us to the next fort?' I asked.

One of the men sitting against the wall – the one with the
rifle – shook his head.

'If you can't we'll have to stay the night here.'

'C'est défendu.'

'Who by?'

'You are a civilian.'

'Nobody's going to make me sit out there on the road and
have my throat cut.'

'Are you French?'

Only one man had spoken. The other sat with his head
turned sideways, watching the slit in the wall. He could have
seen nothing but a postcard of sky: he seemed to be listening
and I began to listen too. The silence became full of sound:

noises you couldn't put a name to – a crack, a creak, a rustle, something like a cough, and a whisper. Then I heard Pyle: he must have come to the foot of the ladder. 'You all right, Thomas?'

'Come up,' I called back. He began to climb the ladder and the silent soldier shifted his sten gun – I don't believe he'd heard a word of what we'd said: it was an awkward, jumpy movement. I realized that fear had paralysed him. I rapped out at him like a sergeant-major, 'Put that gun down!' and I used the kind of French obscenity I thought he would recognize. He obeyed me automatically. Pyle came up into the room. I said, 'We've been offered the safety of the tower till morning.'

'Fine,' Pyle said. His voice was a little puzzled. He said, 'Oughtn't one of those mugs to be on sentry?'

'They prefer not to be shot at. I wish you'd brought something stronger than lime-juice.'

'I guess I will next time,' Pyle said.

'We've got a long night ahead.' Now that Pyle was with me, I didn't hear the noises. Even the two soldiers seemed to have relaxed a little.

'What happens if the Viets attack them?' Pyle asked.

'They'll fire a shot and run. You read it every morning in the *Extrême Orient*. "A post south-west of Saigon was temporarily occupied last night by the Vietminh".'

'It's a bad prospect.'

'There are forty towers like this between us and Saigon. The chances always are that it's the other chap who's hurt.'

'We could have done with those sandwiches,' Pyle said. 'I do think one of them should keep a look-out.'

'He's afraid a bullet might look in.' Now that we too had settled on the floor, the Vietnamese relaxed a little. I felt some sympathy for them: it wasn't an easy job for a couple of ill-trained men to sit up here night after night, never sure of when the Viets might creep up on the road through the fields of paddy. I said to Pyle, 'Do you think they know they are fighting for Democracy? We ought to have York Harding here to explain it to them.'

'You always laugh at York,' said Pyle.

'I laugh at anyone who spends so much time writing about what doesn't exist – mental concepts.'

'They exist for him. Haven't you got any mental concepts? God, for instance?'

'I've no reason to believe in a God. Do you?'

'Yes. I'm a Unitarian.'

'How many hundred million Gods do people believe in? Why, even a Roman Catholic believes in quite a different God when he's scared or happy or hungry.'

'Maybe, if there is a God, he'd be so vast he'd look different to everyone.'

'Like the great Buddha in Bangkok,' I said. 'You can't see all of him at once. Anyway *he* keeps still.'

'I guess you're just trying to be tough,' Pyle said. 'There's something you must believe in. Nobody can go on living without some belief.'

'Oh, I'm not a Berkeleian. I believe my back's against this wall. I believe there's a sten gun over there.'

'I didn't mean that.'

'I believe what I report, which is more than most of your correspondents do.'

'Cigarette?'

'I don't smoke – except opium. Give one to the guards. We'd better stay friends with them.' Pyle got up and lit their cigarettes and came back. I said, 'I wish cigarettes had a symbolic significance like salt.'

'Don't you trust them?'

'No French officer,' I said, 'would care to spend the night alone with two scared guards in one of these towers. Why, even a platoon have been known to hand over their officers. Sometimes the Viets have a better success with a megaphone than a bazooka. I don't blame them. They don't believe in anything either. You and your like are trying to make a war with the help of people who just aren't interested.'

'They don't want Communism.'

'They want enough rice,' I said. 'They don't want to be shot at. They want one day to be much the same as another. They don't want our white skins around telling them what they want.'

'If Indo-China goes . . .'

'I know the record. Siam goes. Malaya goes. Indonesia goes. What does "go" mean? If I believed in your God and another life, I'd bet my future harp against your golden crown that in five hundred years there may be no New York or London, but they'll be growing paddy in these fields, they'll be carrying their produce to market on long poles wearing their pointed hats. The small boys will be sitting on the buffaloes. I like the buffaloes, they don't like our smell, the smell of Europeans. And remember – from a buffalo's point of view you are a European too.'

'They'll be forced to believe what they are told, they won't be allowed to think for themselves.'

'Thought's a luxury. Do you think the peasant sits and thinks of God and Democracy when he gets inside his mud hut at night?'

'You talk as if the whole country were peasant. What about the educated? Are they going to be happy?'

'Oh no,' I said, 'we've brought them up in *our* ideas. We've taught them dangerous games, and that's why we are waiting here, hoping we don't get our throats cut. We deserve to have them cut. I wish your friend York was here too. I wonder how he'd relish it.'

'York Harding's a very courageous man. Why, in Korea . . .'

'He wasn't an enlisted man, was he? He had a return ticket. With a return ticket courage becomes an intellectual exercise, like a monk's flagellation. How much can I stick? Those poor devils can't catch a plane home. Hi,' I called to them, 'what are your names?' I thought that knowledge somehow would bring them into the circle of our conversation. They didn't answer: just lowered back at us behind the stumps of their cigarettes. 'They think we are French,' I said.

'That's just it,' Pyle said. 'You shouldn't be against York, you should be against the French. Their colonialism.'

'Isms and ocracies. Give me facts. A rubber planter beats his labourer – all right, I'm against him. He hasn't been instructed to do it by the Minister of the Colonies. In France I expect he'd beat his wife. I've seen a priest, so poor he hasn't a change of trousers, working fifteen hours a day from hut to hut in a cholera epidemic, eating nothing but rice and salt fish, saying his Mass with an old cup – a wooden platter. I don't believe in God and yet I'm for that priest. Why don't you call that colonialism?'

'It *is* colonialism. York says it's often the good administrators who make it hard to change a bad system.'

'Anyway the French are dying every day – that's not a mental concept. They aren't leading these people on with half-lies like your politicians – and ours. I've been in India, Pyle, and I know the harm liberals do. We haven't a liberal party any more – liberalism's infected all the other parties. We are all either liberal conservatives or liberal socialists: we all have a good conscience. I'd rather be an exploiter who fights for what he exploits, and dies with it. Look at the history of Burma. We go and invade the country: the local tribes support us: we are victorious: but like you Americans we weren't colonialists in those days. Oh no, we made peace with the king and we handed him back his province and left our allies to be crucified and sawn in two. They were innocent. They thought we'd stay. But we were liberals and we didn't want a bad conscience.'

'That was a long time ago.'

'We shall do the same thing here. Encourage them and leave them with a little equipment and a toy industry.'

'Toy industry?'

'Your plastic.'

'Oh yes, I see.'

'I don't know what I'm talking politics for. They don't interest me and I'm a reporter. I'm not *cngagé*.'

'Aren't you?' Pyle said.

'For the sake of an argument – to pass this bloody night, that's all. I don't take sides. I'll be still reporting, whoever wins.'

'If they win, you'll be reporting lies.'

'There's usually a way round, and I haven't noticed much regard for truth in our papers either.'

I think the fact of our sitting there talking encouraged the two soldiers: perhaps they thought the sound of our white voices – for voices have a colour too, yellow voices sing and black voices gargle, while ours just speak – would give an impression of numbers and keep the Viets away. They picked up their pans and began to eat again, scraping with their chopsticks, eyes watching Pyle and me over the rim of the pan.

'So you think we've lost?'

'That's not the point,' I said. 'I've no particular desire to see you win. I'd like those two poor buggers there to be happy – that's all. I wish they didn't have to sit in the dark at night scared.'

'You have to fight for liberty.'

'I haven't seen any Americans fighting around here. And as for liberty, I don't know what it means. Ask them.' I called across the floor in French to them. *La liberté – qu'est ce que c'est la liberté?* They sucked in the rice and stared back and said nothing.

Pyle said, 'Do you want everybody to be made in the same mould? You're arguing for the sake of arguing. You're an intellectual. You stand for the importance of the individual as much as I do – or York.'

'Why have we only just discovered it?' I said. 'Forty years ago no one talked that way.'

'It wasn't threatened then.'

'Ours wasn't threatened, oh no, but who cared about the individuality of the man in the paddy field – and who does now? The only man to treat him as a man is the political commissar. He'll sit in his hut and ask his name and listen to his complaints; he'll give up an hour a day to teaching him – it doesn't matter what, he's being treated like a man, like someone of value. Don't go on in the East with that parrot cry about a threat to the individual soul. Here you'd find yourself on the wrong side – it's they who stand for the individual and we just stand for Private 23987, unit in the global strategy.'

'You don't mean half what you are saying.' Pyle said uneasily.

'Probably three quarters. I've been here a long time. You know, it's lucky I'm not *engagé*, there are things I might be tempted to do – because here in the East – well, I don't like

97

Ike. I like – well, these two. This is their country. What's the time? My watch has stopped.'

'It's turned eight-thirty.'

'Ten hours and we can move.'

'It's going to be quite chilly,' Pyle said and shivered. 'I never expected that.'

'There's water all round. I've got a blanket in the car. That will be enough.'

'Is it safe?'

'It's early for the Viets.'

'Let me go.'

'I'm more used to the dark.'

When I stood up the soldiers stopped eating. I told them, *'Je reviens, tout de suite.'* I dangled my legs over the trap door, found the ladder and went down. It is odd how re-assuring conversation is, especially on abstract subjects: it seems to normalize the strangest surroundings. I was no longer scared: it was as though I had left a room and would be returning there to pick up the argument – the watch tower was the rue Catinat, the bar of the Majestic, or even a room off Gordon Square.

I stood below the tower for a minute to get my vision back. There was starlight, but no moonlight. Moonlight reminds me of a mortuary and the cold wash of an unshaded globe over a marble slab, but starlight is alive and never still, it is almost as though someone in those vast spaces is trying to communicate a message of good will, for even the names of the stars are friendly. Venus is any woman we love, the Bears are the bears of childhood, and I suppose the Southern Cross, to those, like my wife, who believe, may be a favourite hymn or a prayer beside the bed. Once I shivered as Pyle had done. But the night was hot enough, only the shallow stretch of water on either side gave a kind of icing to the warmth. I started out towards the car, and for a moment when I stood on the road I thought it was no longer there. That shook my confidence, even after I remembered that it had petered out thirty yards away. I couldn't help walking with my shoulders bent: I felt more unobtrusive that way.

I had to unlock the boot to get the blanket and the click

and squeak startled me in the silence. I didn't relish being the only noise in what must have been a night full of people. With the blanket over my shoulder I lowered the boot more carefully than I had raised it, and then, just as the catch caught, the sky towards Saigon flared with light and the sound of an explosion came rumbling down the road. A bren spat and spat and was quiet again before the rumbling stopped. I thought, 'Somebody's had it,' and very far away heard voices crying with pain or fear or perhaps even triumph. I don't know why, but I had thought all the time of an attack coming from behind, along the road we had passed, and I had a moment's sense of unfairness that the Viets should be there ahead, between us and Saigon. It was as though we had been unconsciously driving towards danger instead of away from it, just as I was now walking in its direction, back towards the tower. I walked because it was less noisy than to run, but my body wanted to run.

At the foot of the ladder I called up to Pyle, 'It's me – Fowler.' (Even then I couldn't bring myself to use my Christian name to him.) The scene inside the hut had changed. The pans of rice were back on the floor; one man held his rifle on his hip and sat against the wall staring at Pyle and Pyle knelt a little way out from the opposite wall with his eyes on the sten gun which lay between him and the second guard. It was as though he had begun to crawl towards it but had been halted. The second guard's arm was extended towards the gun: no one had fought or even threatened, it was like that child's game when you mustn't be seen to move or you are sent back to base to start again.

'What's going on?' I said.

The two guards looked at me and Pyle pounced, pulling the sten to his side of the room.

'Is it a game?' I asked.

'I don't trust him with the gun,' Pyle said, 'if they are coming.'

'Ever used a sten?'

'No.'

'That's fine. Nor have I. I'm glad it's loaded – we wouldn't know how to reload it.'

The guards had quietly accepted the loss of the gun. The one lowered his rifle and laid it across his thighs; the other slumped against the wall and shut his eyes as though like a child he believed himself invisible in the dark. Perhaps he was glad to have no more responsibility. Somewhere far away the bren started again – three bursts and then silence. The second guard screwed his eyes closer shut.

'They don't know we can't use it,' Pyle said.

'They are supposed to be on our side.'

'I thought you didn't have a side.'

'*Touché,*' I said. 'I wish the Viets knew it.'

'What's happening out there?'

I quoted again tomorrow's *Extrême Orient*: 'A post fifty kilometres outside Saigon was attacked and temporarily captured last night by Vietminh irregulars.'

'Do you think it would be safer in the fields?'

'It would be terribly wet.'

'You don't seem worried,' Pyle said.

'I'm scared stiff – but things are better than they might be. They don't usually attack more than three posts in a night. Our chances have improved.'

'What's that?'

It was the sound of a heavy car coming up the road, driving towards Saigon. I went to the rifle slit and looked down, just as a tank went by.

'The patrol,' I said. The gun in the turret shifted now to this side, now to that. I wanted to call out to them, but what was the good? They hadn't room on board for two useless civilians. The earth floor shook a little as they passed, and they had gone. I looked at my watch – eight fifty-one, and waited, straining to read when the light flapped. It was like judging the distance of lightning by the delay before the thunder. It was nearly four minutes before the gun opened up. Once I thought I detected a bazooka replying, then all was quiet again.

'When they come back,' Pyle said, 'we could signal them for a lift to the camp.'

An explosion set the floor shaking. 'If they come back,' I said. 'That sounded like a mine.' When I looked at my watch again it had passed nine fifteen and the tank had not returned. There had been no more firing.

I sat down beside Pyle and stretched out my legs. 'We'd better try to sleep,' I said. 'There's nothing else we can do.'

'I'm not happy about the guards,' Pyle said.

'They are all right so long as the Viets don't turn up. Put the sten under your leg for safety.' I closed my eyes and tried to imagine myself somewhere else – sitting up in one of the fourth-class compartments the German railways ran before Hitler came to power, in the days when one was young and sat up all night without melancholy, when waking dreams were full of hope and not of fear. This was the hour when Phuong always set about preparing my evening pipes. I wondered whether a letter was waiting for me – I hoped not, for I knew what a letter would contain, and so long as none arrived I could day-dream of the impossible.

'Are you asleep?' Pyle asked.

'No.'

'Don't you think we ought to pull up the ladder?'

'I begin to understand why they don't. It's the only way out.'

'I wish that tank would come back.'

'It won't now.'

I tried not to look at my watch except at long intervals, and the intervals were never as long as they had seemed. Nine forty, ten five, ten twelve, ten thirty-two, ten forty-one.

'You awake?' I said to Pyle.

'Yes.'

'What are you thinking about?'

He hesitated. 'Phuong,' he said.

'Yes?'

'I was just wondering what she was doing.'

'I can tell you that. She'll have decided that I'm spending the night at Tanyin – it won't be the first time. She'll be lying on the bed with a joss stick burning to keep away the mosquitoes and she'll be looking at the pictures in an old *Paris-Match*. Like the French she has a passion for the Royal Family.'

He said wistfully, 'It must be wonderful to know exactly,'

and I could imagine his soft dog's eyes in the dark. They ought to have called him Fido, not Alden.

'I don't really know – but it's probably true. There's no good in being jealous when you can't do anything about it. "No barricado for a belly."'

'Sometimes I hate the way you talk, Thomas. Do you know how she seems to me? She seems fresh, like a flower.'

'Poor flower,' I said. 'There are a lot of weeds around.'

'Where did you meet her?'

'She was dancing at the Grand Monde.'

'Dancing,' he exclaimed, as though the idea were painful.

'It's a perfectly respectable profession,' I said. 'Don't worry.'

'You have such an awful lot of experience, Thomas.'

'I have an awful lot of years. When you reach my age ...'

'I've never had a girl,' he said, 'not properly. Not what you'd call a real experience.'

'A lot of energy with your people seems to go into whistling.'

'I've never told anybody else.'

'You're young. It's nothing to be ashamed of.'

'Have you had a lot of women, Fowler?'

'I don't know what a lot means. Not more than four women have had any importance to me – or me to them. The other forty-odd – one wonders why one does it. A notion of hygiene, of one's social obligations, both mistaken.'

'You think they *are* mistaken?'

'I wish I could have those nights back. I'm still in love, Pyle, and I'm a wasting asset. Oh, and there was pride, of course. It takes a long time before we cease to feel proud of being wanted. Though God knows why we should feel it, when we look around and see who is wanted too.'

'You don't think there's anything wrong with me, do you, Thomas?'

'No, Pyle.'

'It doesn't mean I don't *need* it, Thomas, like everybody else. I'm not – odd.'

'Not one of us needs it as much as we say. There's an awful lot of self-hypnosis around. Now I know I need nobody

– except Phuong. But that's a thing one learns with time. I could go a year without one restless night if she wasn't there.'

'But she *is* there,' he said in a voice I could hardly catch.

'One starts promiscuous and ends like one's grandfather, faithful to one woman.'

'I suppose it seems pretty naïve to start that way...'

'No.'

'It's not in the Kinsey Report.'

'That's why it's not naïve.'

'You know, Thomas, it's pretty good being here, talking to you like this. Somehow it doesn't seem dangerous any more.'

'We used to feel that in the blitz,' I said, 'when a lull came. But they always returned.'

'If somebody asked you what your deepest sexual experience had been, what would you say?'

I knew the answer to that. 'Lying in bed early one morning and watching a woman in a red dressing-gown brush her hair.'

'Joe said it was being in bed with a Chink and a negress at the same time.'

'I'd have thought that one up too when I was twenty.'

'Joe's fifty.'

'I wonder what mental age they gave him in the war.'

'Was Phuong the girl in the red dressing-gown?'

I wished that he hadn't asked that question.

'No,' I said, 'that woman came earlier. When I left my wife.'

'What happened?'

'I left her, too.'

'Why?'

Why indeed? 'We are fools,' I said, 'when we love. I was terrified of losing her. I thought I saw her changing – I don't know if she really was, but I couldn't bear the uncertainty any longer. I ran towards the finish just like a coward runs towards the enemy and wins a medal. I wanted to get death over.'

'Death?'

'It was a kind of death. Then I came east.'

'And found Phuong?'

'Yes.'

'But don't you find the same thing with Phuong?'

'Not the same. You see, the other one loved me. I was afraid of losing love. Now I'm only afraid of losing Phuong.' Why had I said that, I wondered? He didn't need encouragement from me.

'But she loves you, doesn't she?'

'Not like that. It isn't in their nature. You'll find that out. It's a cliché to call them children – but there's one thing which is childish. They love you in return for kindness, security, the presents you give them – they hate you for a blow or an injustice. They don't know what it's like – just walking into a room and loving a stranger. For an aging man, Pyle, it's very secure – she won't run away from home so long as the home is happy.'

I hadn't meant to hurt him. I only realized I had done it when he said with muffled anger, 'She might prefer greater security or more kindness.'

'Perhaps.'

'Aren't you afraid of that?'

'Not so much as I was of the other.'

'Do you love her at all?'

'Oh yes, Pyle, yes. But that other way I've only loved once.'

'In spite of the forty-odd women,' he snapped at me.

'I'm sure it's below the Kinsey average. You know, Pyle, women don't want virgins. I'm not sure we do, unless we are a pathological type.'

'I didn't mean I was a virgin,' he said. All my conversations with Pyle seemed to take grotesque directions. Was it because of his sincerity that they so ran off the customary rails? His conversation never took the corners.

'You can have a hundred women and still be a virgin, Pyle. Most of your G.I.s who were hanged for rape in the war were virgins. We don't have so many in Europe. I'm glad. They do a lot of harm.'

'I just don't understand you, Thomas.'

'It's not worth explaining. I'm bored with the subject anyway. I've reached the age when sex isn't the problem so much as old age and death. I wake up with these in mind and not a woman's body. I just don't want to be alone in my last decade, that's all. I wouldn't know what to think about all day long. I'd sooner have a woman in the same room – even one I didn't love. But if Phuong left me, would I have the energy to find another? . . .'

'If that's all she means to you . . .'

'All, Pyle? Wait until you're afraid of living ten years alone with no companion and a nursing home at the end of it. Then you'll start running in any direction, even away from that girl in the red dressing-gown, to find someone, anyone, who will last until you are through.'

'Why don't you go back to your wife, then?'

'It's not easy to live with someone you've injured.'

A sten gun fired a long burst – it couldn't have been more than a mile away. Perhaps a nervous sentry was shooting at shadows: perhaps another attack had begun. I hoped it was an attack – it increased our chances.

'Are you scared, Thomas?'

'Of course I am. With all my instincts. But with my reason I know it's better to die like this. That's why I came east. Death stays with you.' I looked at my watch. It had gone eleven. An eight-hour night and then we could relax. I said, 'We seem to have talked about pretty nearly everything except God. We'd better leave him to the small hours.'

'You don't believe in Him, do you?'

'No.'

'Things to me wouldn't make sense without Him.'

'They don't make sense to me with him.'

'I read a book once . . .'

I never knew what book Pyle had read. (Presumably it wasn't York Harding or Shakespeare or the anthology of contemporary verse or *The Physiology of Marriage* – perhaps it was *The Triumph of Life*.) A voice came right into the tower with us, it seemed to speak from the shadows by the trap – a hollow megaphone voice saying something in Vietnamese. 'We're for it,' I said. The two guards listened, their faces turned to the rifle slit, their mouths hanging open.

'What is it?' Pyle asked.

Walking to the embrasure was like walking through the voice. I looked quickly out: there was nothing to be seen – I couldn't even distinguish the road and when I looked back into the room the rifle was pointed, I wasn't sure whether at me or at the slit. But when I moved round the wall the rifle wavered, hesitated, kept me covered: the voice went on saying the same thing over again. I sat down and the rifle was lowered.

'What's he saying?' Pyle asked.

'I don't know. I expect they've found the car and are telling these chaps to hand us over or else. Better pick up that sten before they make up their minds.'

'He'll shoot.'

'He's not sure yet. When he is he'll shoot anyway.'

Pyle shifted his leg and the rifle came up.

'I'll move along the wall,' I said. 'When his eyes waver get him covered.'

Just as I rose the voice stopped: the silence made me jump. Pyle said sharply, 'Drop your rifle.' I had just time to wonder whether the sten was unloaded – I hadn't bothered to look – when the man threw his rifle down.

I crossed the room and picked it up. Then the voice began again – I had the impression that no syllable had changed. Perhaps they used a record. I wondered when the ultimatum would expire.

'What happens next?' Pyle asked, like a schoolboy watching a demonstration in the laboratory: he didn't seem personally concerned.

'Perhaps a bazooka, perhaps a Viet.'

Pyle examined his sten. 'There doesn't seem any mystery about this,' he said. 'Shall I fire a burst?'

'No, let them hesitate. They'd rather take the post without firing and it gives us time. We'd better clear out fast.'

'They may be waiting at the bottom.'

'Yes.'

The two men watched us – I write men, but I doubt whether they had accumulated forty years between them. 'And these?' Pyle asked, and he added with a shocking directness, 'Shall I shoot them?' Perhaps he wanted to try the sten.

'They've done nothing.'

'They were going to hand us over.'

'Why not?' I said. 'We've no business here. It's their country.'

I unloaded the rifle and laid it on the floor. 'Surely you're not leaving that,' he said.

'I'm too old to run with a rifle. And this isn't my war. Come on.'

It wasn't my war, but I wished those others in the dark knew that as well. I blew the oil-lamp out and dangled my legs over the trap, feeling for the ladder. I could hear the guards whispering to each other like crooners, in their language like a song. 'Make straight ahead,' I told Pyle, 'aim for the rice. Remember there's water – I don't know how deep. Ready?'

'Yes.'

'Thanks for the company.'

'Always a pleasure,' Pyle said.

I heard the guards moving behind us: I wondered if they had knives. The megaphone voice spoke peremptorily as though offering a last chance. Something shifted softly in the dark below us, but it might have been a rat. I hesitated. 'I wish to God I had a drink,' I whispered.

'Let's go.'

Something was coming up the ladder: I heard nothing, but the ladder shook under my feet.

'What's keeping you?' Pyle said.

I don't know why I thought of it as something, that silent stealthy approach. Only a man could climb a ladder, and yet I couldn't think of it as a man like myself – it was as though an animal were moving in to kill, very quietly and certainly with the remorselessness of another kind of creation. The ladder shook and shook and I imagined I saw its eyes glaring upwards. Suddenly I could bear it no longer and I jumped, and there was nothing there at all but the spongy ground, which took my ankle and twisted it as a hand might have done. I could hear Pyle coming down the ladder; I realized I had been a frightened fool who could not recognize his own trembling, and I had believed I was tough and unimaginative, all that a truthful observer and reporter should be. I got on my feet and nearly fell again with the pain. I started out for

107

the field dragging one foot after me and heard Pyle coming behind me. Then the bazooka shell burst on the tower and I was on my face again.

4

'Are you hurt?' Pyle said.

'Something hit my leg. Nothing serious.'

'Let's get on,' Pyle urged me. I could just see him because he seemed to be covered with a fine white dust. Then he simply went out like a picture on the screen when the lamps of the projector fail: only the soundtrack continued. I got gingerly up on to my good knee and tried to rise without putting any weight on my bad left ankle, and then I was down again breathless with pain. It wasn't my ankle: something had happened to my left leg. I couldn't worry – pain took away care. I lay very still on the ground hoping that pain wouldn't find me again. I even held my breath, as one does with toothache. I didn't think about the Viets who would soon be searching the ruins of the tower: another shell exploded on it – they were making quite sure before they came in. What a lot of money it costs, I thought as the pain receded, to kill a few human beings – you can kill horses so much cheaper. I can't have been fully conscious, for I began to think I had strayed into a knacker's yard which was the terror of my childhood in the small town where I was born. We used to think we heard the horses whinnying with fear and the explosion of the painless killer.

It was some while since the pain had returned, now that I was lying still and holding my breath – that seemed to me just as important. I wondered quite lucidly whether perhaps I ought to crawl towards the fields. The Viets might not have time to search far. Another patrol would be out by now trying to contact the crew of the first tank. But I was more afraid of the pain than of the partisans, and I lay still. There was no sound anywhere of Pyle: he must have reached the fields. Then I heard someone weeping. It came from the direction of the tower, or what had been the tower. It wasn't like a man weeping: it was like a child who is frightened of the dark and yet afraid to scream. I supposed it was one of the two boys –

108

perhaps his companion had been killed. I hoped that the Viets wouldn't cut his throat. One shouldn't fight a war with children and a little curled body in a ditch came back to mind. I shut my eyes – that helped to keep the pain away, too, and waited. A voice called something I didn't understand. I almost felt I could sleep in this darkness and loneliness and absence of pain.

Then I heard Pyle whispering, 'Thomas. Thomas.' He had learnt footcraft quickly; I had not heard him return.

'Go away,' I whispered back.

He found me then and lay down flat beside me. 'Why didn't you come? Are you hurt?'

'My leg. I think it's broken.'

'A bullet?'

'No, no. Log of wood. Stone. Something from the tower. It's not bleeding.'

'You've got to make an effort.'

'Go away, Pyle. I don't want to, it hurts too much.'

'Which leg?'

'Left.'

He crept round to my side and hoisted my arm over his shoulder. I wanted to whimper like the boy in the tower and then I was angry, but it was hard to express anger in a whisper. 'God damn you, Pyle, leave me alone. I want to stay.'

'You can't.'

He was pulling me half on to his shoulder and the pain was intolerable. 'Don't be a bloody hero. I don't want to go.'

'You've got to help,' he said, 'or we are both caught.'

'You . . .'

'Be quiet or they'll hear you.' I was crying with vexation – you couldn't use a stronger word. I hoisted myself against him and let my left leg dangle – we were like awkward contestants in a three-legged race and we wouldn't have stood a chance if, at the moment we set off, a bren had not begun to fire in quick short bursts somewhere down the road towards the next tower. Perhaps a patrol was pushing up or perhaps they were completing their score of three towers destroyed. It covered the noise of our slow and clumsy flight.

I'm not sure whether I was conscious all the time: I think for the last twenty yards Pyle must have almost carried my weight. He said, 'Careful here. We are going in.' The dry rice rustled around us and the mud squelched and rose. The water was up to our waists when Pyle stopped. He was panting and a catch in his breath made him sound like a bull-frog.

'I'm sorry,' I said.

'Couldn't leave you,' Pyle said.

The first sensation was relief; the water and mud held my leg tenderly and firmly like a bandage, but soon the cold set us chattering. I wondered whether it had passed midnight yet; we might have six hours of this if the Viets didn't find us.

'Can you shift your weight a little,' Pyle said, 'just for a moment?' And my unreasoning irritation came back – I had no excuse for it but the pain. I hadn't asked to be saved, or to have death so painfully postponed. I thought with nostalgia of my couch on the hard dry ground. I stood like a crane on one leg trying to relieve Pyle of my weight, and when I moved, the stalks of rice tickled and cut and crackled.

'You saved my life there,' I said, and Pyle cleared his throat for the conventional response, 'so that I could die here. I prefer dry land.'

'Better not talk,' Pyle said as though to an invalid.

'Who the hell asked you to save my life? I came east to be killed. It's like your damned impertinence . . .' I staggered in the mud and Pyle hoisted my arm around his shoulder. 'Ease it off,' he said.

'You've been seeing war-films. We aren't a couple of marines and you can't win a war-medal.'

'Sh-sh.' Footsteps could be heard, coming down to the edge of the field. The bren up the road stopped firing and there was no sound except the footsteps and the slight rustle of the rice when we breathed. Then the footsteps halted: they only seemed the length of a room away. I felt Pyle's hand on my good side pressing me slowly down; we sank together into the mud very slowly so as to make the least disturbance of the rice. On one knee, by straining my head backwards, I could just keep my mouth out of the water. The pain came back to my leg and I thought, 'If I faint here I drown' – I

110

had always hated and feared the thought of drowning. Why can't one choose one's death? There was no sound now: perhaps twenty feet away they were waiting for a rustle, a cough, a sneeze – 'Oh God,' I thought, 'I'm going to sneeze.' If only he had left me alone, I would have been responsible only for my own life – not his – and he wanted to live. I pressed my free fingers against my upper lip in that trick we learn when we are children playing at Hide and Seek, but the sneeze lingered, waiting to burst, and silent in the darkness the others waited for the sneeze. It was coming, coming, came . . .

But in the very second that my sneeze broke, the Viets opened with stens, drawing a line of fire through the rice – it swallowed my sneeze with its sharp drilling like a machine punching holes through steel. I took a breath and went under – so instinctively one avoids the loved thing, coquetting with death, like a woman who demands to be raped by her lover. The rice was lashed down over our heads and the storm passed. We came up for air at the same moment and heard the footsteps going away back towards the tower.

'We've made it,' Pyle said, and even in my pain I wondered what we'd made: for me, old age, an editor's chair, loneliness; and as for him, I know now that he spoke prematurely. Then in the cold we settled down to wait. Along the road to Tanyin a bonfire burst into life: it burnt merrily like a celebration.

'That's my car,' I said.

Pyle said, 'It's a shame, Thomas. I hate to see waste.'

'There must have been just enough petrol in the tank to set it going. Are you as cold as I am, Pyle?'

'I couldn't be colder.'

'Suppose we get out and lie flat on the road?'

'Let's give them another half hour.'

'The weight's on you.'

'I can stick it, I'm young.' He had meant the claim humorously, but it struck as cold as the mud. I had intended to apologize for the way my pain had spoken, but now it spoke again. 'You're young all right. You can afford to wait, can't you.'

'I don't get you, Thomas.'

111

We had spent what seemed to have been a week of nights together, but he could no more understand me than he could understand French. I said, 'You'd have done better to let me be.'

'I couldn't have faced Phuong,' he said, and the name lay there like a banker's bid. I took it up.

'So it was for her,' I said. What made my jealousy more absurd and humiliating was that it had to be expressed in the lowest of whispers – it had no tone, and jealousy likes histrionics. 'You think these heroics will get her. How wrong you are. If I were dead you could have had her.'

'I didn't mean that,' Pyle said. 'When you are in love you want to play the game, that's all.' That's true, I thought, but not as he innocently means it. To be in love is to see yourself as someone else sees you, it is to be in love with the falsified and exalted image of yourself. In love we are incapable of honour – the courageous act is no more than playing a part to an audience of two. Perhaps I was no longer in love but I remembered.

'If it had been you, I'd have left you,' I said.

'Oh no, you wouldn't, Thomas.' He added with unbearable complacency, 'I know you better than you do yourself.' Angrily I tried to move away from him and take my own weight, but the pain came roaring back like a train in a tunnel and I leant more heavily against him, before I began to sink into the water. He got both arms round me and held me up, and then inch by inch he began to edge me to the bank and the roadside. When he got me there he lowered me flat in the shallow mud below the bank at the edge of the field, and when the pain retreated and I opened my eyes and ceased to hold my breath, I could see only the elaborate cypher of the constellations – a foreign cypher which I couldn't read: they were not the stars of home. His face wheeled over me, blotting them out. 'I'm going down the road, Thomas, to find a patrol.'

'Don't be a fool,' I said. 'They'll shoot you before they know who you are. If the Viets don't get you.'

'It's the only chance. You can't lie in the water for six hours.'

112

'Then lay me in the road.'

'It's no good leaving you the sten?' he asked doubtfully.

'Of course it's not. If you are determined to be a hero, at least go slowly through the rice.'

'The patrol would pass before I could signal it.'

'You don't speak French.'

'I shall call out "*Je suis Franççais*". Don't worry, Thomas. I'll be very careful.' Before I could reply he was out of a whisper's range – he was moving as quietly as he knew how, with frequent pauses. I could see him in the light of the burning car, but no shot came; soon he passed beyond the flames and very soon the silence filled the footprints. Oh yes, he was being careful as he had been careful boating down the river into Phat Diem, with the caution of a hero in a boy's adventure-story, proud of his caution like a Scout's badge and quite unaware of the absurdity and the improbability of his adventure.

I lay and listened for the shots from the Viets or a Legion patrol, but none came – it would probably take him an hour or even more before he reached a tower, if he ever reached it. I turned my head enough to see what remained of our tower, a heap of mud and bamboo and struts which seemed to sink lower as the flames of the car sank. There was peace when the pain went – a kind of Armistice Day of the nerves: I wanted to sing. I thought how strange it was that men of my profession would make only two news-lines out of all this night – it was just a common-or-garden night and I was the only strange thing about it. Then I heard a low crying begin again from what was left of the tower. One of the guards must still be alive.

I thought, 'Poor devil, if we hadn't broken down outside *his* post, he could have surrendered as they nearly all surrendered, or fled, at the first call from the megaphone. But we were there – two white men, and we had the sten and they didn't dare to move. When we left it was too late.' I was responsible for that voice crying in the dark: I had prided myself on detachment, on not belonging to this war, but those wounds had been inflicted by me just as though I had used the sten, as Pyle had wanted to do.

113

I made an effort to get over the bank into the road. I wanted to join him. It was the only thing I could do, to share his pain. But my own personal pain pushed me back. I couldn't hear him any more. I lay still and heard nothing but my own pain beating like a monstrous heart and held my breath and prayed to the God I didn't believe in, 'Let me die or faint. Let me die or faint'; and then I suppose I fainted and was aware of nothing until I dreamed that my eyelids had frozen together and someone was inserting a chisel to prise them apart, and I wanted to warn them not to damage the eyeballs beneath but couldn't speak and the chisel bit through and a torch was shining on my face.

'We made it, Thomas,' Pyle said. I remember that, but I don't remember what Pyle later described to others: that I waved my hand in the wrong direction and told them there was a man in the tower and they had to see to him. Anyway I couldn't have made the sentimental assumption that Pyle made. I know myself, and I know the depth of my selfishness. I cannot be at ease (and to be at ease is my chief wish) if someone else is in pain, visibly or audibly or tactually. Sometimes this is mistaken by the innocent for unselfishness, when all I am doing is sacrificing a small good – in this case postponement in attending to my hurt – for the sake of a far greater good, a peace of mind when I need think only of myself.

They came back to tell me the boy was dead, and I was happy – I didn't even have to suffer much pain after the hypodermic of morphia had bitten my leg.

Chapter 3

1

I CAME slowly up the stairs to the flat in the rue Catinat, pausing and resting on the first landing. The old women gossiped as they always had done, squatting on the floor outside the urinoir, carrying Fate in the lines of their faces as others on the palm. They were silent as I passed and I wondered what they might have told me, if I had known their language, of what had passed while I had been away in the Legion Hospital back on the road towards Tanyin. Somewhere in the tower and the fields I had lost my keys, but I had sent a message to Phuong which she must have received, if she was still there. That 'if' was the measure of my uncertainty. I had had no news of her in hospital, but she wrote French with difficulty, and I couldn't read Vietnamese. I knocked on the door and it opened immediately and everything seemed to be the same. I watched her closely while she asked how I was and touched my splinted leg and gave me her shoulder to lean on, as though one could lean with safety on so young a plant. I said, 'I'm glad to be home.'

She told me that she had missed me, which of course was what I wanted to hear: she always told me what I wanted to hear, like a coolie answering questions, unless by accident. Now I awaited the accident.

'How have you amused yourself?' I asked.

'Oh, I have seen my sister often. She has found a post with the Americans.'

'She has, has she? Did Pyle help?'

'Not Pyle, Joe.'

'Who's Joe?'

'You know him. The Economic Attaché.'

'Oh, of course, Joe.'

He was a man one always forgot. To this day I cannot describe him, except his fatness and his powdered clean-shaven cheeks and his big laugh; all his identity escapes me – except that he was called Joe. There are some men whose names are always shortened.

With Phuong's help I stretched myself on the bed. 'Seen any movies?' I asked.

'There is a very funny one at the Catinat,' and immediately she began to tell me the plot in great detail, while I looked around the room for the white envelope that might be a telegram. So long as I didn't ask, I could believe that she had forgotten to tell me, and it might be there on the table by the typewriter, or on the wardrobe, perhaps put for safety in the cupboard-drawer where she kept her collection of scarves.

'The postmaster – I think he was the postmaster, but he may have been the mayor – followed them home, and he borrowed a ladder from the baker and he climbed through Corinne's window, but, you see, she had gone into the next room with François, but he did not hear Mme Bompierre coming and she came in and saw him at the top of the ladder and thought . . .'

'Who was Mme Bompierre?' I asked, turning my head to see the wash-basin, where sometimes she propped reminders among the lotions.

'I told you. She was Corinne's mother and she was looking for a husband because she was a widow . . .'

She sat on the bed and put her hand inside my shirt. 'It was very funny,' she said.

'Kiss me, Phuong.' She had no coquetry. She did at once what I asked and she went on with the story of the film. Just so she would have made love if I had asked her to, straight away, peeling off her trousers without question, and after-wards have taken up the thread of Mme Bompierre's story and the postmaster's predicament.

'Has a call come for me?'

'Yes.'

'Why didn't you give it me?'

'It is too soon for you to work. You must lie down and rest.'

'This may not be work.'

She gave it me and I saw that it had been opened. It read:

116

'Four hundred words background wanted effect de Lattre's departure on military and political situation.'

'Yes,' I said. 'It *is* work. How did you know? Why did you open it?'

'I thought it was from your wife. I hoped that it was good news.'

'Who translated it for you?'

'I took it to my sister.'

'If it had been bad news would you have left me, Phuong?'

She rubbed her hand across my chest to reassure me, not realizing that it was words this time I required, however untrue. 'Would you like a pipe? There *is* a letter for you. I think perhaps it is from her.'

'Did you open that too?'

'I don't open your letters. Telegrams are public. The clerks read them.'

This envelope was among the scarves. She took it gingerly out and laid it on the bed. I recognized the hand-writing. 'If this is bad news what will you . . . ?' I knew well that it could be nothing else but bad. A telegram might have meant a sudden act of generosity: a letter could only mean explanation, justification . . . so I broke off my question, for there was no honesty in asking for the kind of promise no one can keep.

'What are you afraid of?' Phuong asked, and I thought, 'I'm afraid of the loneliness, of the Press Club and the bed-sitting room, I'm afraid of Pyle.'

'Make me a brandy-and-soda,' I said. I looked at the beginning of the letter, 'Dear Thomas,' and the end, 'Affectionately, Helen,' and waited for the brandy.

'It is from *her*?'

'Yes.' Before I read it I began to wonder whether at the end I should lie or tell the truth to Phuong.

' Dear Thomas,

' I was not surprised to get your letter and to know that you were not alone. You are not a man, are you? to remain alone for very long. You pick up women like your coat picks up dust. Perhaps I would feel more sympathy with your case if I didn't feel that you

117

would find consolation very easily when you return to London. I don't suppose you'll believe me, but what gives me pause and prevents me cabling you a simple No is the thought of the poor girl. We are apt to be more involved than you are.'

I had a drink of brandy. I hadn't realized how open the sexual wounds remain over the years. I had carelessly – not choosing my words with skill – set hers bleeding again. Who could blame her for seeking my own scars in return? When we are unhappy we hurt.

'Is it bad?' Phuong asked.

'A bit hard,' I said. 'But she has the right . . .' I read on.

'I always believed you loved Anne more than the rest of us until you packed up and went. Now you seem to be planning to leave another woman because I can tell from your letter that you don't really expect a "favourable" reply. "I'll have done my best " – aren't you thinking that? What would you do if I cabled " Yes "? Would you actually marry her? (I have to write " her " – you don't tell me her name.) Perhaps you would. I suppose like the rest of us you are getting old and don't like living alone. I feel very lonely myself sometimes. I gather Anne has found another companion. But you left her in time.'

She had found the dried scab accurately. I drank again. An issue of blood – the phrase came into my mind.

'Let me make you a pipe,' Phuong said.

'Anything,' I said, 'anything.'

'That is one reason why I ought to say No. (We don't need to talk about the religious reason, because you've never understood or believed in that.) Marriage doesn't prevent you leaving a woman, does it? It only delays the process, and it would be all the more unfair to the girl in this case if you lived with her as long as you lived with me. You would bring her back to England where she would be lost and a stranger, and when you left her, how terribly abandoned she would feel. I don't suppose she even uses a knife and fork, does she? I'm being harsh because I'm thinking of her good more than I am of yours. But, Thomas dear, I do think of yours too.'

I felt physically sick. It was a long time since I had received a letter from my wife. I had forced her to write it and I could

118

feel her pain in every line. Her pain struck at my pain: we were back at the old routine of hurting each other. If only it were possible to love without injury – fidelity isn't enough: I had been faithful to Anne and yet I had injured her. The hurt is in the act of possession: we are too small in mind and body to possesss another person without pride or to be possessed without humiliation. In a way I was glad that my wife had struck out at me again – I had forgotten her pain for too long, and this was the only kind of recompense I could give her. Unfortunately the innocent are always involved in any conflict. Always, everywhere, there is some voice crying from a tower.

Phuong lit the opium lamp. 'Will she let you marry me?'

'I don't know yet.'

'Doesn't she say?'

'If she does, she says it very slowly.'

I thought, 'How much you pride yourself on being *dégagé*, the reporter, not the leader-writer, and what a mess you make behind the scenes. The other kind of war is more innocent than this. One does less damage with a mortar.'

'If I go against my deepest conviction and say "Yes", would it even be good for you? You say you are being recalled to England and I can realize how you will hate that and do anything to make it easier. I can see you marrying after a drink too many. The first time we really tried – you as well as me – and we failed. One doesn't try so hard the second time. You say it will be the end of life to lose this girl. Once you used exactly that phrase to me – I could show you the letter, I have it still – and I suppose you wrote in the same way to Anne. You say that we've always tried to tell the truth to each other, but, Thomas, your truth is always so temporary. What's the good of arguing with you, or trying to make you see reason? It's easier to act as my faith tells me to act – as you think unreasonably – and simply to write: I don't believe in divorce: my religion forbids it, and so the answer, Thomas, is no – no.'

There was another half-page, which I didn't read, before 'Affectionately, Helen'. I think it contained news of the weather and an old aunt of mine I loved.

I had no cause for complaint, and I had expected this reply. There was a lot of truth in it. I only wished that she had not thought aloud at quite such length, when the thoughts hurt her as well as me.

'She says "No"?'

I said with hardly any hesitation, 'She hasn't made up her mind. There's still hope.'

Phuong laughed. '–You say "hope" with such a long face.' She lay at my feet like a dog on a crusader's tomb, preparing the opium, and I wondered what I should say to Pyle. When I had smoked four pipes I felt more ready for the future and I told her the hope was a good one – my wife was consulting a lawyer. Any day now I would get the telegram of release.

'It would not matter so much. You could make a settlement,' she said, and I could hear her sister's voice speaking through her mouth.

'I have no savings,' I said. 'I can't outbid Pyle.'

'Don't worry. Something may happen. There are always ways,' she said. 'My sister says you could take out a life-insurance,' and I thought how realistic it was of her not to minimize the importance of money and not to make any great and binding declarations of love. I wondered how Pyle over the years would stand that hard core, for Pyle was a romantic; but then of course in his case there would be a good settlement, the hardness might soften like an unused muscle when the need for it vanished. The rich had it both ways.

That evening, before the shops had closed in the rue Catinat, Phuong bought three more silk scarves. She sat on the bed and displayed them to me, exclaiming at the bright colours, filling a void with her singing voice, and then folding them carefully she laid them with a dozen others in her drawer: it was as though she were laying the foundation of a modest settlement. And I laid the crazy foundation of mine, writing a letter that very night to Pyle with the unreliable clarity and foresight of opium. This was what I wrote – I found it again the other day tucked into York Harding's *Rôle of the West*. He must have been reading the book when my letter arrived. Perhaps he had used it as a bookmark and then not gone on reading.

'Dear Pyle,' I wrote, and was tempted for the only time to

write, 'Dear Alden,' for, after all, this was a bread-and-butter letter of some importance and it differed from other bread-and-butter letters in containing a falsehood:

'Dear Pyle, I have been meaning to write from the hospital to say thank you for the other night. You certainly saved me from an uncomfortable end. I'm moving about again now with the help of a stick – I broke apparently in just the right place and age hasn't yet reached my bones and made them brittle. We must have a party together some time to celebrate.' (My pen stuck on that word, and then, like an ant meeting an obstacle, went round it by another route.) 'I've got something else to celebrate and I know you will be glad of this, too, for you've always said that Phuong's interests were what we both wanted. I found a letter from my wife waiting when I got back, and she's more or less agreed to divorce me. So you don't need to worry any more about Phuong' – it was a cruel phrase, but I didn't realize the cruelty until I read the letter over and then it was too late to alter. If I were going to scratch that out, I had better tear the whole letter up.

'Which scarf do you like best?' Phuong asked. 'I love the yellow.'

'Yes. The yellow. Go down to the hotel and post this letter for me.'

She looked at the address. 'I could take it to the Legation. It would save a stamp.'

'I would rather you posted it.'

Then I lay back and in the relaxation of the opium I thought, 'At least she won't leave me now before I go, and perhaps, somehow, tomorrow, after a few more pipes, I shall think of a way to remain.'

2

Ordinary life goes on – that has saved many a man's reason. Just as in an air-raid it proved impossible to be frightened all the time, so under the bombardment of routine jobs, of chance encounters, of impersonal anxieties, one lost for hours together the personal fear. The thoughts of the coming April, of leaving Indo-China, of the hazy future without Phuong, were affected by the day's telegrams, the bulletins of the Vietnam Press, and by the illness of my assistant, an Indian called Dominguez (his family had come from Goa by way of Bombay) who had attended in my place the less important Press Conferences, kept a sensitive ear open to the tones of gossip and rumour, and took my messages to the cable-offices and the censorship. With the help of Indian traders, particularly in the north, in Haiphong, Nam Dinh and Hanoi, he ran his own personal Intelligence Service for my benefit, and I think he knew more accurately than the French High Command the location of Vietminh battalions within the Tonkin delta.

And because we never used our information except when it became news, and never passed any reports to the French intelligence, he had the trust and the friendship of several Vietminh agents hidden in Saigon-Cholon. The fact that he was an Asiatic, in spite of his name, unquestionably helped.

I was fond of Dominguez. Where other men carry their pride like a skin-disease on the surface, sensitive to the least touch, his pride was deeply hidden, and reduced to the smallest proportion possible, I think, for any human being. All that you encountered in daily contact with him was gentleness and humility and an absolute love of truth: you would have had to be married to him to discover the pride. Perhaps truth and humility go together; so many lies come from our pride – in my profession a reporter's pride, the desire to file a better story than the other man's, and it was Dominguez who helped me not to care – to withstand all those telegrams from home asking why I had not covered so and so's story or the report of someone else which I knew to be untrue.

Now that he was ill I realized how much I owed him – why, he would even see that my car was full of petrol, and yet never once, with a phrase or a look, had he encroached on my private life. I believe he was a Roman Catholic, but I had no evidence for it beyond his name and the place of his origin – for all I knew from his conversation, he might have worshipped Krishna or gone on annual pilgrimages, pricked by a wire frame, to the Batu Caves. Now his illness came like a mercy, reprieving me from the treadmill of private anxiety. It was I now who had to attend the wearisome Press Conferences and hobble to my table at the Continental for a gossip with my colleagues; but I was less capable than Dominguez of telling truth from falsehood, and so I formed the habit of calling in on him in the evenings to discuss what I had heard. Sometimes one of his Indian friends was there, sitting beside the narrow iron bed in the lodgings Dominguez shared in one of the meaner streets off the Boulevard Galliéni. He would sit up straight in his bed with his feet tucked under him so that you had less the impression of visiting a sick man than of being received by a rajah or a priest. Sometimes when his fever was bad his face ran with sweat, but he never lost the clarity of his thought. It was as though his illness were happening to another person's body. His landlady kept a jug of fresh lime by his side, but I never saw him take a drink – perhaps that would have been to admit that it was his own thirst, and his own body which suffered.

Of all the days that I visited him I remember one in particular. I had given up asking him how he was for fear that the question sounded like a reproach, and it was always he who inquired with great anxiety about my health and apologized for the stairs I had to climb. Then he said, 'I would like you to meet a friend of mine. He has a story you should listen to.'

'Yes.'

'I have his name written down because I know you find it difficult to remember Chinese names. We must not use it, of course. He has a warehouse on the Quai Mytho for junk metal.'

'Important?'

'It might be.'

'Can you give me an idea?'

'I would rather you heard from him. There is something strange, but I don't understand it.' The sweat was pouring down his face, but he just let it run as though the drops were alive and sacred – there was that much of the Hindu in him, he would never have endangered the life of a fly. He said, 'How much do you know of your friend Pyle?'

'Not very much. Our tracks cross, that's all. I haven't seen him since Tanyin.'

123

'What job does he do?'

'Economic Mission, but that covers a multitude of sins. I think he's interested in home-industries – I suppose with an American business tie-up. I don't like the way they keep the French fighting and cut out their business at the same time.'

'I heard him talking the other day at a party the Legation was giving to visiting Congressmen. They had put him on to brief them.'

'God help Congress,' I said, 'he hasn't been in the country six months.'

'He was talking about the old colonial powers – England and France, and how you two couldn't expect to win the confidence of the Asiatics. That was where America came in now with clean hands.'

'Hawaii, Puerto Rico,' I said, 'New Mexico.'

'Then someone asked him some stock question about the chances of the Government here ever beating the Vietminh and he said a Third Force could do it. There was always a Third Force to be found free from Communism and the taint of colonialism – national democracy he called it; you only had to find a leader and keep him safe from the old colonial powers.'

'It's all in York Harding,' I said. 'He had read it before he came out here. He talked about it his first week and he's learned nothing.'

'He may have found his leader,' Dominguez said.

'Would it matter?'

'I don't know. I don't know what he does. But go and talk to my friend on the Quai Mytho.'

I went home to leave a note for Phuong in the rue Catinat and then drove down past the port as the sun set. The tables and chairs were out on the *quai* beside the steamers and the grey naval boats, and the little portable kitchens burned and bubbled. In the Boulevard de la Somme the hairdressers were busy under the trees and the fortune-tellers squatted against the walls with their soiled packs of cards. In Cholon you were in a different city where work seemed to be just beginning rather than petering out with the daylight. It was like driving into a pantomime set: the long vertical Chinese signs and the bright lights and the crowd of extras led you into the wings, where everything was suddenly so much darker and quieter. One such wing took me down again to the *quai* and a huddle of sampans, where the warehouses yawned in the shadow and no one was about.

I found the place with difficulty and almost by accident, the godown gates were open, and I could see the strange Picasso shapes of the junk-pile by the light of an old lamp: bedsteads, bathtubs, ashcans, the bonnets of cars, stripes of old colour where the light hit. I walked down a narrow track carved in the iron quarry and called out for Mr Chou, but there was no reply. At the end of the godown a stair led up to what I supposed might be Mr Chou's house – I had apparently been directed to the back door, and I supposed that Dominguez had his reasons. Even the staircase was lined with junk, pieces of scrap-iron which might come in useful one day in this jackdaw's nest of a house. There was one big room on the landing and a whole family sat and lay about in it with the effect of a camp which might be struck at any moment. Small tea-cups stood about everywhere and there were lots of cardboard boxes full of unidentifiable objects and fibre suitcases ready strapped; there was an old lady sitting on a big bed, two boys and two girls, a baby crawling on the floor, three middle-aged women in old brown peasant-trousers and jackets, and two old men in a corner in blue silk mandarin coats playing mah jongg. They paid no attention to my coming; they played rapidly, identifying each piece by touch, and the noise was like shingle turning on a beach after a wave withdraws. No one paid any more attention than they did; only a cat leapt on to a cardboard box and a lean dog sniffed at me and withdrew.

'Monsieur Chou?' I asked, and two of the women shook their heads, and still no one regarded me, except that one of the women rinsed out a cup and poured tea from a pot which had been resting warm in its silk-lined box. I sat down on the end of the bed next the old lady and a girl brought me the cup: it was as though I had been absorbed into the community with the cat and the dog – perhaps they had turned up the first time as fortuitously as I had. The baby crawled across the floor and pulled at my laces and no one reproved it: one didn't in the East reprove children. Three commercial calendars were hanging on the walls, each with a girl in gay Chinese costume with bright pink cheeks. There was a big mirror mysteriously lettered Café de la Paix – perhaps it had got caught up accidentally in the junk: I felt caught up in it myself.

I drank slowly the green bitter tea, shifting the handleless cup from palm to palm as the heat scorched my fingers, and I wondered how long I ought to stay. I tried the family once in French, asking when they expected Monsieur Chou to return, but no one replied: they had probably not understood. When my cup was empty they refilled it and continued their own occupations: a woman ironing, a girl sewing, the two boys at their lessons, the old lady looking at her feet, the tiny crippled feet of old China – and the dog watching the cat, which stayed on the cardboard boxes.

I began to realize how hard Dominguez worked for his lean living.

A Chinese of extreme emaciation came into the room. He seemed to take up no room at all: he was like the piece of greaseproof paper that divides the biscuits in a tin. The only thickness he had was in his striped flannel pyjamas. 'Monsieur Chou?' I asked.

He looked at me with the indifferent gaze of a smoker: the sunken cheeks, the baby wrists, the arms of a small girl – many years and many pipes had been needed to whittle him down to these dimensions. I said, 'My friend, Monsieur Dominguez, said that you had something to show me. You *are* Monsieur Chou?'

Oh yes, he said, he was Monsieur Chou and waved me courteously back to my seat. I could tell that the object of my coming had been lost somewhere within the smoky corridors of his skull. I would have a cup of tea? he was much honoured by my visit. Another cup was rinsed on to the floor and put like a live coal into my hands – the ordeal by tea. I commented on the size of his family.

He looked round with faint surprise as though he had never seen it in that light before. 'My mother,' he said, 'my wife, my sister, my uncle, my brother, my children, my aunt's children.' The baby had rolled away from my feet and lay on its back kicking and crowing. I wondered to whom it belonged. No one seemed young enough – or old enough – to have produced that.

I said, 'Monsieur Dominguez told me it was important.'

'Ah, Monsieur Dominguez. I hope Monsieur Dominguez is well?'

'He has had a fever.'

'It is an unhealthy time of year.' I wasn't convinced that he even remembered who Dominguez was. He began to cough, and under his pyjama jacket, which had lost two buttons, the tight skin twanged like a native drum.

'You should see a doctor yourself,' I said. A newcomer joined us – I hadn't heard him enter. He was a young man neatly dressed in European clothes. He said in English, 'Mr Chou has only one lung.'

'I am very sorry . . .'

'He smokes one hundred and fifty pipes every day.'

'That sounds a lot.'

'The doctor says it will do him no good, but Mr Chou feels much happier when he smokes.'

I made an understanding grunt.

'If I may introduce myself, I am Mr Chou's manager.'

'My name is Fowler. Mr Dominguez sent me. He said that Mr Chou had something to tell me.'

'Mr Chou's memory is very much impaired. Will you have a cup of tea?'

'Thank you, I have had three cups already.' It sounded like a question and an answer in a phrase-book.

Mr Chou's manager took the cup out of my hand and held it out to one of the girls, who after spilling the dregs on the floor again refilled it.

'That is not strong enough,' he said, and took it and tasted it himself, carefully rinsed it and refilled it from a second teapot. 'That is better?' he asked.

'Much better.'

Mr Chou cleared his throat, but it was only for an immense expectoration into a tin spittoon decorated with pink blooms.

The baby rolled up and down among the tea-dregs and the cat leapt from a cardboard box on to a suitcase.

'Perhaps it would be better if you talked to me,' the young man said. 'My name is Mr Heng.'

'If you would tell me . . .'

'We will go down to the warehouse,' Mr Heng said. 'It is quieter there.'

I put out my hand to Mr Chou, who allowed it to rest between his palms with a look of bewilderment, then gazed around the crowded room as though he were trying to fit me in. The sound of the turning shingle receded as we went down the stairs. Mr Heng said, 'Be careful. The last step is missing,' and he flashed a torch to guide me.

We were back among the bedsteads and the bathtubs and Mr Heng led the way down a side aisle. When he had gone about twenty paces he stopped and shone his light on to a small iron drum. He said, 'Do you see that?'

'What about it?'

He turned it over and showed the trade mark: 'Diolacton.'

'It still means nothing to me.'

He said, 'I had two of those drums here. They were picked up with other junk at the garage of Mr Phan-Van-Muoi. You know him?'

'No, I don't think so.'

'His wife is a relation of General Thé.'

'I still don't quite see . . . ?'

'Do you know what this is?' Mr Heng asked, stooping and lifting a long concave object like a stick of celery which glistened chromium in the light of his torch.

'It might be a bath-fixture.'

'It is a mould,' Mr Heng said. He was obviously a man who took a tiresome pleasure in giving instruction. He paused for me to show my ignorance again. 'You understand what I mean by a mould?'

'Oh yes, of course, but I still don't follow . . .'

'This mould was made in U.S.A. Diolacton is an American trade name. You begin to understand?'

'Frankly, no.'

'There is a flaw in the mould. That was why it was thrown away. But it should not have been thrown away with the junk – nor the drum either. That was a mistake. Mr Muoi's manager came here personally. I could not find the mould, but I let him have back the other drum. I said it was all I had, and he told me he needed them for storing chemicals. Of course, he did not ask for the mould – that would have given too much away – but he had a good search. Mr Muoi himself called later at the American Legation and asked for Mr Pyle.'

'You seem to have quite an Intelligence Service,' I said. I still couldn't imagine what it was all about.

'I asked Mr Chou to get in touch with Mr Dominguez.'

'You mean you've established a kind of connection between Pyle and the General,' I said. 'A very slender one. It's not news anyway. Everybody here goes in for Intelligence.'

Mr Heng beat his heel against the black iron drum and the sound reverberated among the bedsteads. He said, 'Mr Fowler, you are English. You are neutral. You have been fair to all of us. You can sympathize if some of us feel strongly on whatever side.'

I said, 'If you are hinting that you are a Communist, or a Vietminh, don't worry. I'm not shocked. I have no politics.'

'If anything unpleasant happens here in Saigon, it will be blamed on us. My Committee would like you to take a fair view. That is why I have shown you this and this.'

'What is Diolacton?' I said. 'It sounds like condensed milk.'

'It has something in common with milk.' Mr Heng shone his torch inside the drum. A little white powder lay like dust on the bottom. 'It is one of the American plastics,' he said.

'I heard a rumour that Pyle was importing plastics for toys.' I picked up the mould and looked at it. I tried in my mind to divine its shape. This was not how the object itself would look: this was the image in a mirror, reversed.

'Not for toys,' Mr Heng said.

'It is like parts of a rod.'

'The shape is unusual.'

'I can't see what it could be for.'

Mr Heng turned away. 'I only want you to remember what

129

you have seen,' he said, walking back in the shadows of the junk-pile. 'Perhaps one day you will have a reason for writing about it. But you must not say you saw the drum here.'

'Nor the mould?' I asked.

'Particularly not the mould.'

3

It is not easy the first time to meet again one who has saved as they put it – one's life. I had not seen Pyle while I was in the Legion Hospital, and his absence and silence, easily accountable (for he was more sensitive to embarrassment than I), sometimes worried me unreasonably, so that at night before my sleeping drug had soothed me I would imagine him going up my stairs, knocking at my door, sleeping in my bed. I had been unjust to him in that, and so I had added a sense of guilt to my other more formal obligation. And then I suppose there was also the guilt of my letter. (What distant ancestors had given me this stupid conscience? Surely they were free of it when they raped and killed in their palaeolithic world.)

Should I invite my saviour to dinner, I sometimes wondered, or should I suggest a meeting for a drink in the bar of the Continental? It was an unusual social problem, perhaps depending on the value one attributed to one's life. A meal and a bottle of wine or a double whisky? – it had worried me for some days until the problem was solved by Pyle himself, who came and shouted at me through my closed door. I was sleeping through the hot afternoon, exhausted by the morning's effort to use my leg, and I hadn't heard his knock.

'Thomas, Thomas.' The call dropped into a dream I was having of walking down a long empty road looking for a turning which never came. The road unwound like a tape-machine with a uniformity that would never have altered if the voice hadn't broken in -- first of all like a voice crying in pain from a tower and then suddenly a voice speaking to me personally, 'Thomas, Thomas.'

Under my breath I said, 'Go away, Pyle. Don't come near me. I don't want to be saved.'

'Thomas.' He was hitting at my door, but I lay possum as

130

though I were back in the rice-field and he was an enemy. Suddenly I realized that the knocking had stopped, someone was speaking in a low voice outside and someone was replying. Whispers are dangerous. I couldn't tell who the speakers were. I got carefully off the bed and with the help of my stick reached the door of the other room. Perhaps I had moved too hurriedly and they had heard me, because a silence grew outside. Silence like a plant put out tendrils: it seemed to grow under the door and spread its leaves in the room where I stood. It was a silence I didn't like, and I tore it apart by flinging the door open. Phuong stood in the passage and Pyle had his hands on her shoulders: from their attitude they might have parted from a kiss.

'Why, come in,' I said, 'come in.'

'I couldn't make you hear,' Pyle said.

'I was asleep at first, and then I didn't want to be disturbed. But I *am* disturbed, so come in.' I said in French to Phuong, 'Where did you pick him up?'

'Here. In the passage,' she said. 'I heard him knocking, so I ran upstairs to let him in.'

'Sit down,' I said to Pyle. 'Will you have some coffee?'

'No, and I don't want to sit down, Thomas.'

'I must. This leg gets tired. You got my letter?'

'Yes. I wish you hadn't written it.'

'Why?'

'Because it was a pack of lies. I trusted you, Thomas.'

'You shouldn't trust anyone when there's a woman in the case.'

'Then you needn't trust me after this. I'll come sneaking up here when you go out, I'll write letters in typewritten envelopes. Maybe I'm growing up, Thomas.' But there were tears in his voice, and he looked younger than he had ever done. 'Couldn't you have won without lying?'

'No. This is European duplicity, Pyle. We have to make up for our lack of supplies. I must have been clumsy though. How did you spot the lies?'

'It was her sister,' he said. 'She's working for Joe now. I saw her just now. She knows you've been called home.'

'Oh, that,' I said with relief. 'Phuong knows it too.'

'And the letter from your wife? Does Phuong know about that? Her sister's seen it.'

'How?'

'She came here to meet Phuong when you were out yesterday and Phuong showed it to her. You can't deceive her. She reads English.'

'I see.' There wasn't any point in being angry with anyone – the offender was too obviously myself, and Phuong had probably only shown the letter as a kind of boast – it wasn't a sign of mistrust.

'You knew all this last night?' I asked Phuong.

'Yes.'

'I noticed you were quiet.' I touched her arm. 'What a fury you might have been, but you're Phuong – you are no fury.'

'I had to think,' she said, and I remembered how waking in the night I had told from the irregularity of her breathing that she was not asleep. I'd put my arm out to her and asked her '*Le caucheman*?' She used to suffer from nightmares when she first came to the rue Catinat, but last night she had shaken her head at the suggestion: her back was turned to me and I had moved my leg against her – the first move in the formula of intercourse. I had noticed nothing wrong even then.

'Can't you explain, Thomas, why . . .'

'Surely it's obvious enough. I wanted to keep her.'

'At any cost to her?'

'Of course.'

'That's not love.'

'Perhaps it's not your way of love, Pyle.'

'I want to protect her.'

'I don't. She doesn't need protection. I want her around, I want her in my bed.'

'Against her will?'

'She wouldn't stay against her will, Pyle.'

'She can't love you after this.' His ideas were as simple as that. I turned to look for her. She had gone through to the bedroom and was pulling the counterpane straight where I had lain; then she took one of her picture books from a shelf and sat on the bed as though she were quite unconcerned with our talk. I could tell what book it was – a pictorial record of

132

the Queen's life. I could see upside-down the state coach on the way to Westminster.

'Love's a Western word,' I said. 'We use it for sentimental reasons or to cover up an obsession with one woman. These people don't suffer from obsessions. You're going to be hurt, Pyle, if you aren't careful.'

'I'd have beaten you up if it wasn't for that leg.'

'You should be grateful to me – and Phuong's sister, of course. You can go ahead without scruples now – and you are very scrupulous in some ways, aren't you, when it doesn't come to plastics.'

'Plastics?'

'I hope to God you know what you are doing there. Oh, I know your motives are good, they always are.' He looked puzzled and suspicious. 'I wish sometimes you had a few bad motives, you might understand a little more about human beings. And that applies to your country too, Pyle.'

'I want to give her a decent life. This place -- smells.'

'We keep the smell down with joss sticks. I suppose you'll offer her a deep freeze and a car for herself and the newest television set and . . .'

'And children,' he said.

'Bright young American citizens ready to testify.'

'And what will you give her? You weren't going to take her home.'

'No, I'm not that cruel. Unless I can afford her a return ticket.'

'You'll just keep her as a comfortable lay until you leave.'

'She's a human being, Pyle. She's capable of deciding.'

'On faked evidence. And a child at that.'

'She's no child. She's tougher than you'll ever be. Do you know the kind of polish that doesn't take scratches? That's Phuong. She can survive a dozen of us. She'll get old, that's all. She'll suffer from childbirth and hunger and cold and rheumatism, but she'll never suffer like we do from thoughts, obsessions -- she won't scratch, she'll only decay.' But even while I made my speech and watched her turn the page (a family group with Princess Anne), I knew I was inventing a character just as much as Pyle was. One never knows another

133

human being; for all I could tell, she was as scared as the rest of us: she didn't have the gift of expression, that was all. And I remembered that first tormenting year when I had tried so passionately to understand her, when I had begged her to tell me what she thought and had scared her with my unreasoning anger at her silences. Even my desire had been a weapon, as though when one plunged one's sword towards the victim's womb, she would lose control and speak.

'You've said enough,' I told Pyle. 'You know all there is to know. Please go.'

'Phuong,' he called.

'Monsieur Pyle?' she inquired, looking up from the scrutiny of Windsor Castle, and her formality was comic and reassuring at that moment.

'He's cheated you.'

'*Je ne comprends pas.*'

'Oh, go away,' I said. 'Go to your Third Force and York Harding and the Rôle of Democracy. Go away and play with plastics.'

Later I had to admit that he had carried out my instructions to the letter.

PART THREE

Chapter 1

1

It was nearly a fortnight after Pyle's death before I saw Vigot again. I was going up the Boulevard Charner when his voice called to me from Le Club. It was the restaurant most favoured in those days by members of the Sureté, who, as a kind of defiant gesture to those who hated them, would lunch and drink on the ground-floor while the general public fed upstairs out of the reach of a partisan with a hand-grenade. I joined him and he ordered me a vermouth cassis. 'Play for it?'

'If you like,' and I took out my dice for the ritual game of *Quatre Cent Vingt-et-un*. How those figures and the sight of dice bring back to mind the war-years in Indo-China. Anywhere in the world when I see two men dicing I am back in the streets of Hanoi or Saigon or among the blasted buildings of Phat Diem, I see the parachutists, protected like caterpillars by their strange markings, patrolling by the canals, I hear the sound of the mortars closing in, and perhaps I see a dead child.

'*Sans vaseline,*' Vigot said, throwing a four-two-one. He pushed the last match towards me. The sexual jargon of the game was common to all the Sureté; perhaps it had been invented by Vigot and taken up by his junior officers, who hadn't however taken up Pascal. '*Sous-lieutenant.*' Every game you lost raised you a rank – you played till one or other became a captain or a commandant. He won the second game as well and while he counted out the matches, he said, 'We've found Pyle's dog.'

'Yes?'

'I suppose it had refused to leave the body. Anyway they cut its throat. It was in the mud fifty yards away. Perhaps it dragged itself that far.'

'Are you still interested?'

'The American Minister keeps bothering us. We don't have

137

the same trouble, thank God, when a Frenchman is killed. But then those cases don't have rarity value.'

We played for the division of matches and then the real game started. It was uncanny how quickly Vigot threw a four-two-one. He reduced his matches to three and I threw the lowest score possible. '*Nanette*,' Vigot said, pushing me over two matches. When he had got rid of his last match he said, '*Capitaine*,' and I called the waiter for drinks. 'Does anybody ever beat you?' I asked.

'Not often. Do you want your revenge?'

'Another time. What a gambler you could be, Vigot. Do you play any other game of chance?'

He smiled miserably, and for some reason I thought of that blonde wife of his who was said to betray him with his junior officers.

'Oh well,' he said, 'there's always the biggest of all.'

'The biggest?'

'"Let us weigh the gain and loss," he quoted, "in wagering that God is, let us estimate these two chances. If you gain, you gain all; if you lose you lose nothing."'

I quoted Pascal back at him – it was the only passage I remembered. '"Both he who chooses heads and he who chooses tails are equally at fault. They are both in the wrong. True course is not to wager at all."'

'"Yes; but you must wager. It is not optional. You are embarked." You don't follow your own principles, Fowler. You're *engagé*, like the rest of us.'

'Not in religion.'

'I wasn't talking about religion. As a matter of fact,' he said, 'I was thinking about Pyle's dog.'

'Oh.'

'Do you remember what you said to me – about finding clues on its paws, analysing the dirt and so on?'

'And you said you weren't Maigret or Lecoq.'

'I've not done so badly after all,' he said. 'Pyle usually took the dog with him when he went out, didn't he?'

'I suppose so.'

'It was too valuable to let it stray by itself?'

'It wouldn't be very safe. They eat chows, don't they, in this country?' He began to put the dice in his pocket. 'My dice, Vigot.'

'Oh, I'm sorry. I was thinking . . .'

'Why did you say I was *engagé*?'

'When did you last see Pyle's dog, Fowler?'

'God knows. I don't keep an engagement-book for dogs.'

'When are you due to go home?'

'I don't know exactly.' I never like giving information to the police. It saves them trouble.

'I'd like – tonight – to drop in and see you. At ten? If you will be alone.'

'I'll send Phuong to the cinema.'

'Things all right with you again – with her?'

'Yes.'

'Strange. I got the impression that you are – well – unhappy.'

'Surely there are plenty of possible reasons for that, Vigot.' I added bluntly, 'You should know.'

'Me?'

'You're not a very happy man yourself.'

'Oh, I've nothing to complain about. "A ruined house is not miserable."'

'What's that?'

'Pascal again. It's an argument for being proud of misery. "A tree is not miserable."'

'What made you into a policeman, Vigot?'

'There were a number of factors. The need to earn a living, a curiosity about people, and – yes, even that, a love of Gaboriau.'

'Perhaps you ought to have been a priest.'

'I didn't read the right authors for that – in those days.'

'You still suspect me, don't you, of being concerned?'

He rose and drank what was left of his vermouth cassis.

'I'd like to talk to you, that's all.'

I thought after he had turned and gone that he had looked at me with compassion, as he might have looked at some prisoner, for whose capture he was responsible, undergoing his sentence for life.

I *had* been punished. It was as though Pyle, when he left my flat, had sentenced me to so many weeks of uncertainty. Every time that I returned home it was with the expectation of disaster. Sometimes Phuong would not be there, and I found it impossible to settle to any work till she returned, for I always wondered whether she would ever return. I would ask her where she had been (trying to keep anxiety or suspicion out of my voice) and sometimes she would reply the market or the shops and produce her piece of evidence (even her readiness to confirm her story seemed at that period unnatural), and sometimes it was the cinema, and the stub of her ticket was there to prove it, and sometimes it was her sister's – that was where I believed she met Pyle. I made love to her in those days savagely as though I hated her, but what I hated was the future. Loneliness lay in my bed and I took loneliness into my arms at night. She didn't change; she cooked for me, she made my pipes, she gently and sweetly laid out her body for my pleasure (but it was no longer a pleasure), and just as in those early days I wanted her mind, now I wanted to read her thoughts, but they were hidden away in a language I couldn't speak. I didn't want to question her. I didn't want to make her lie (as long as no lie was spoken openly I could pretend that we were the same to each other as we had always been), but suddenly my anxiety would speak for me, and I said, 'When did you last see Pyle?'

She hesitated – or was it that she was really thinking back? 'When we came here,' she said.

I began – almost unconsciously – to run down everything that was American. My conversation was full of the poverty of American literature, the scandals of American politics, the beastliness of American children. It was as though she were being taken away from me by a nation rather than by a man. Nothing that America could do was right. I became a bore on the subject of America, even with my French friends who were ready enough to share my antipathies. It was as if I had been betrayed, but one is not betrayed by an enemy.

It was just at that time that the incident occurred of the

bicycle bombs. Coming back from the Imperial Bar to an empty flat (was she at the cinema or with her sister?) I found that a note had been pushed under the door. It was from Dominguez. He apologized for being still sick and asked me to be outside the big store at the corner of the Boulevard Charner around ten-thirty the next morning. He was writing at the request of Mr Chou, but I suspected that Mr Heng was the more likely to require my presence.

The whole affair, as it turned out, was not worth more than a paragraph, and a humorous paragraph at that. It bore no relation to the sad and heavy war in the north, those canals in Phat Diem choked with the grey days-old bodies, the pounding of the mortars, the white glare of napalm. I had been waiting for about a quarter of an hour by a stall of flowers when a truck-load of police drove up with a grinding of brakes and a squeal of rubber from the direction of the Sureté Headquarters in the rue Catinat; the men disembarked and ran for the store, as though they were charging a mob, but there was no mob – only a zareba of bicycles. Every large building in Saigon is fenced in by them – no university city in the West contains so many bicycle-owners. Before I had time to adjust my camera the comic and inexplicable action had been accomplished. The police had forced their way among the bicycles and emerged with three which they carried over their heads into the boulevard and dropped into the decorative fountain. Before I could intercept a single policeman they were back in their truck and driving hard down the Boulevard Bonnard.

'*Operation Bicyclette*,' a voice said. It was Mr Heng.

'What is it?' I asked. 'A practice? For what?'

'Wait a while longer,' Mr Heng said.

A few idlers began to approach the fountain, where one wheel stuck up like a buoy as though to warn shipping away from the wrecks below: a policeman crossed the road shouting and waving his hands.

'Let's have a look,' I said.

'Better not,' Mr Heng said, and examined his watch. The hands stood at four minutes past eleven.

'You're fast,' I said.

141

'It always gains.' And at that moment the fountain exploded over the pavement. A bit of decorative coping struck a window and the glass fell like the water in a bright shower. Nobody was hurt. We shook the water and glass from our clothes. A bicycle wheel hummed like a top in the road, staggered and collapsed. 'It must be just eleven,' Mr Heng said.

'What on earth . . . ?'

'I thought you would be interested,' Mr Heng said. 'I *hope* you were interested.'

'Come and have a drink?'

'No, I am sorry. I must go back to Mr Chou's, but first let me show you something.' He led me to the bicycle park and unlocked his own machine. 'Look carefully.'

'A Raleigh,' I said.

'No, look at the pump. Does it remind you of anything?' He smiled patronizingly at my mystification and pushed off. Once he turned and waved his hand, pedalling towards Cholon and the warehouse of junk. At the Sureté, where I went for information, I realized what he meant. The mould I had seen in his warehouse had been shaped like a half-section of a bicycle-pump. That day all over Saigon innocent bicycle-pumps had proved to contain bombs which had gone off at the stroke of eleven, except where the police, acting on information that I suspect emanated from Mr Heng, had been able to anticipate the explosions. It was all quite trivial – ten explosions, six people slightly injured, and God knows how many bicycles. My colleagues – except for the correspondent of the *Extrême Orient,* who called it an 'outrage' – knew they could only get space by making fun of the affair. 'Bicycle Bombs' made a good headline. All of them blamed the Communists. I was the only one to write that the bombs were a demonstration on the part of General Thé, and my account was altered in the office. The General wasn't news. You couldn't waste space by identifying him. I sent a message of regret through Dominguez to Mr Heng – I had done my best. Mr Heng sent a polite verbal reply. It seemed to me then that he – or his Vietminh Committee – had been unduly sensitive; no one held the affair seriously against the Communists.

Indeed, if anything could have done so, it would have given them the reputation for a sense of humour. 'What'll they think of next?' people said at parties, and the whole absurd affair was symbolized for me too in the bicycle-wheel gaily spinning like a top in the middle of the boulevard. I never even mentioned to Pyle what I had heard of his connection with the General. Let him play harmlessly with plastic moulds: it might keep his mind off Phuong. All the same, because I happened to be in the neighbourhood one evening, because I had nothing better to do, I called in at Mr Muoi's garage.

It was a small, untidy place, not unlike a junk warehouse itself, in the Boulevard de la Somme. A car was jacked up in the middle of the floor with its bonnet open, gaping like the cast of some pre-historic animal in a provincial museum which nobody ever visits. I don't believe anyone remembered it was there. The floor was littered with scraps of iron and old boxes – the Vietnamese don't like throwing anything away, any more than a Chinese cook partitioning a duck into seven courses will dispense with so much as a claw. I wondered why anybody had so wastefully disposed of the empty drums and the damaged mould – perhaps it was a theft by an employee making a few piastres, perhaps somebody had been bribed by the ingenious Mr Heng.

Nobody seemed about, so I went in. Perhaps, I thought, they are keeping away for a while in case the police call. It was possible that Mr Heng had some contact in the Sureté, but even then it was unlikely that the police would act. It was better from their point of view to let people assume that the bombs were Communist.

Apart from the car and the junk strewn over the concrete floor there was nothing to be seen. It was difficult to picture how the bombs could have been manufactured at Mr Muoi's. I was very vague about how one turned the white dust I had seen in the drum into plastic, but surely the process was too complex to be carried out here, where even the two petrol pumps in the street seemed to be suffering from neglect. I stood in the entrance and looked out into the street. Under the trees in the centre of the boulevard the barbers were at work: a scrap of mirror nailed to a tree-trunk caught the flash of the sun. A girl went by at a trot under her mollusc hat carrying two baskets slung on a pole. The fortune-teller squatting against the wall of Simon Frères had found a customer, an old man with a whisp of beard like Ho Chi Minh's who watched impassively the shuffling and turning of the ancient cards. What possible future had he got that was worth a piastre? In the Boulevard de la Somme you lived in the open; everybody here knew all about Mr Muoi, but the police had no key which would unlock their confidence. This was the level of life where everything was known, but you couldn't step down to that level as you could step into the street. I remembered the old women gossiping on our landing beside the communal lavatory: they heard everything too, but I didn't know what they knew.

I went back into the garage and entered a small office at the back. There was the usual Chinese commercial calendar, a littered desk – price-lists and a bottle of gum and an adding-machine, some paper-clips, a teapot and three cups and a lot of unsharpened pencils, and for some reason an unwritten picture-postcard of the Eiffel Tower. York Harding might write in graphic abstractions about the Third Force, but this was what it came down to – this was It. There was a door in the back wall; it was locked, but the key was on the desk among the pencils. I opened the door and went through.

I was in a small shed about the size of the garage. It contained one piece of machinery that at first sight seemed like a cage of rods and wires furnished with innumerable perches to hold some wingless adult bird – it gave the impression of being tied up with old rags, but the rags had probably been used for cleaning when Mr Muoi and his assistants had been called away. I found the name of a manufacture. – somebody in Lyons and a patent number – patenting what? I switched on the current and the old machine came alive: the rods had a purpose – the contraption was like an old man gathering his last vital force, pounding down his fist, pounding down ... This thing was still a press, though in its own sphere it must have belonged to the same era as the nickelodeon, but I suppose that in this country where nothing was ever wasted, and where everything might be expected to come one day to

144

finish its career (I remembered seeing that ancient movie *The Great Train Robbery* jerking its way across a screen, giving entertainment, in a back-street in Nam Dinh), the press was still employable.

I examined the press more closely; there were traces of a white powder. Diolacton, I thought, something in common with milk. There was no sign of a drum or a mould. I went back into the office and into the garage. I felt like giving the old car a pat on the mudguard; it had a long wait ahead of it, perhaps, but it too one day . . . Mr Muoi and his assistants were probably by this time somewhere among the rice-fields on the way to the sacred mountain where General Thé had his headquarters. When now at last I raised my voice and called 'Monsieur Muoi!' I could imagine I was far away from the garage and the boulevard and the barbers, back among those fields where I had taken refuge on the road to Tanyin. 'Monsieur Muoi!' I could see a man turn his head among the stalks of rice.

I walked home and up on my landing the old women burst into their twitter of the hedges which I could understand no more than the gossip of the birds. Phuong was not in – only a note to say that she was with her sister. I lay down on the bed – I still tired easily – and fell asleep. When I woke I saw the illuminated dial of my alarm pointing to one twenty-five and I turned my head expecting to find Phuong asleep beside me. But the pillow was undented. She must have changed the sheet that day – it carried the coldness of the laundry. I got up and opened the drawer where she kept her scarves, and they were not there. I went to the bookshelf – the pictorial Life of the Royal Family had gone too. She had taken her dowry with her.

In the moment of shock there is little pain; pain began about three a.m. when I began to plan the life I had still somehow to live and to remember memories in order somehow to eliminate them. Happy memories are the worst, and I tried to remember the unhappy. I was practised. I had lived all this before. I knew I could do what was necessary, but I was so much older – I felt I had little energy left to reconstruct.

145

I went to the American Legation and asked for Pyle. It was necessary to fill in a form at the door and give it to a military policeman. He said, 'You haven't put the purpose of the visit.'

'He'll know,' I said.

'You're by appointment, then?'

'You can put it that way if you like.'

'Seems silly to you, I guess, but we have to be very careful. Some strange types come around here.'

'So I've heard.' He shifted his chewing-gum to another side and entered the lift. I waited. I had no idea what to say to Pyle. This was a scene I had never played before. The policeman returned. He said grudgingly, 'I guess you can go up. Room 12A. First floor.'

When I entered the room I saw that Pyle wasn't there. Joe sat behind the desk: the Economic Attaché: I still couldn't remember his surname. Phuong's sister watched me from behind a typing desk. Was it triumph that I read in those brown acquisitive eyes?

'Come in, come in, Tom,' Joe called boisterously. 'Glad to see you. How's your leg? We don't often get a visit from you to our little outfit. Pull up a chair. Tell me how you think the new offensive's going. Saw Granger last night at the Continental. He's for the north again. That boy's *keen*. Where there's news there's Granger. Have a cigarette. Help yourself. You know Miss Hei? Can't remember all these names – too hard for an old fellow like me. I call her "Hi, there!" – she likes it. None of this stuffy colonialism. What's the gossip of the market, Tom? You fellows certainly do keep your ears to the ground. Sorry to hear about your leg. Alden told me . . .'

'Where's Pyle?'

'Oh, Alden's not in the office this morning. Guess he's at home. Does a lot of his work at home.'

'I know what he does at home.'

'That boy's keen. Eh, what's that you said?'

'Anyway, I know one of the things he does at home.'

'I don't catch on, Tom. Slow Joe – that's me. Always was. Always will be.'

'He sleeps with my girl – your typist's sister.'

'I don't know what you mean.'

'Ask her. She fixed it. Pyle's taken my girl.'

'Look here, Fowler, I thought you'd come here on business. We can't have scenes in the office, you know.'

'I came here to see Pyle, but I suppose he's hiding.'

'Now, you're the very last man who ought to make a remark like that. After what Alden did for you.'

'Oh yes, yes, of course. He saved my life, didn't he? But I never asked him to.'

'At great danger to himself. That boy's got guts.'

'I don't care a damn about his guts. There are other parts of his body that are more à propos.'

'Now we can't have any innuendoes like that, Fowler, with a lady in the room.'

'The lady and I know each other well. She failed to get her rake-off from me, but she's getting it from Pyle. All right. I know I'm behaving badly, and I'm going to go on behaving badly. This is a situation where people do behave badly.'

'We've got a lot of work to do. There's a report on the rubber output . . .'

'Don't worry, I'm going. But just tell Pyle if he phones that I called. He might think it polite to return the visit.' I said to Phuong's sister, 'I hope you've had the settlement witnessed by the notary public and the American Consul and the Church of Christ Scientist.'

I went into the passage. There was a door opposite me marked Men. I went in and locked the door and sitting with my head against the cold wall I cried. I hadn't cried until now. Even their lavatories were air-conditioned, and presently the temperate tempered air dried my tears as it dries the spit in your mouth and the seed in your body.

4

I left affairs in the hands of Dominguez and went north. At Haiphong I had friends in the Squadron Gascogne, and I would spend hours in the bar up at the airport, or playing bowls on the gravel-path outside. Officially I was at the front:

I could qualify for keenness with Granger, but it was of no more value to my paper than had been my excursion to Phat Diem. But if one writes about war, self-respect demands that occasionally one shares the risks.

It wasn't easy to share them for even the most limited period, since orders had gone out from Hanoi that I was to be allowed only on horizontal raids – raids in this war as safe as a journey by bus, for we flew above the range of the heavy machine-gun; we were safe from anything but a pilot's error or a fault in the engine. We went out by time-table and came home by time-table: the cargoes of bombs sailed diagonally down and the spiral of smoke blew up from the road-junction or the bridge, and then we cruised back for the hour of the aperitif and drove our iron bowls across the gravel.

One morning in the mess in the town, as I drank brandies-and-sodas with a young officer who had a passionate desire to visit Southend Pier, orders for a mission came in. 'Like to come?' I said yes. Even a horizontal raid would be a way of killing time and killing thought. Driving out to the airport he remarked, 'This is a vertical raid.'

'I thought I was forbidden . . .'

'So long as you write nothing about it. It will show you a piece of country up near the Chinese border you will not have seen before. Near Lai Chau.'

'I thought all was quiet there – and in French hands?'

'It was. They captured this place two days ago. Our para-chutists are only a few hours away. We want to keep the Viets head down in their holes until we have recaptured the post. It means low diving and machine-gunning. We can only spare two planes – one's on the job now. Ever dive-bombed before?'

'No.'

'It is a little uncomfortable when you are not used to it.'

The Gascogne Squadron possessed only small B.26 bombers – the French called them prostitutes because with their short wing-span they had no visible means of support. I was crammed on to a little metal pad the size of a bicycle seat with my knees against the navigator's back. We came up the Red River, slowly climbing, and the Red River at this hour was really red. It was as though one had gone far back in time and saw it with the old geographer's eyes who had named it first, at just such an hour when the late sun filled it from bank to bank; then we turned away at 9,000 feet towards the Black River, really black, full of shadows, missing the angle of the light, and the huge majestic scenery of gorge and cliff and jungle wheeled around and stood upright below us. You could have dropped a squadron into those fields of green and grey and left no more trace than a few coins in a harvest-field. Far ahead of us a small plane moved like a midge. We were taking over.

We circled twice above the tower and the green-encircled village, then corkscrewed up into the dazzling air. The pilot – who was called Trouin – turned to me and winked. On his wheel were the studs that controlled the gun and the bomb-chamber. I had that loosening of the bowels, as we came into position for the dive, that accompanies any new experience – the first dance, the first dinner-party, the first love. I was reminded of the Great Racer at the Wembley Exhibition when it came to the top of the rise – there was no way to get out: you were trapped with your experience. On the dial I had just time to read 3,000 metres when we drove down. All was feeling now, nothing was sight. I was forced up against the navigator's back: it was as though something of enormous weight were pressing on my chest. I wasn't aware of the moment when the bombs were released; then the gun chattered and the cockpit was full of the smell of cordite, and the weight was off my chest as we rose, and it was the stomach that fell away, spiralling down like a suicide to the ground we had left. For forty seconds Pyle had not existed: even loneliness hadn't existed. As we climbed in a great arc I could see the smoke through the side window pointing at me. Before the second dive I felt fear – fear of humiliation, fear of vomiting over the navigator's back, fear that my ageing lungs would not stand the pressure. After the tenth dive I was aware only of irritation – the affair had gone on too long, it was time to go home. And again we shot steeply up out of machine-gun range and swerved away and the smoke pointed. The village was surrounded on all sides by mountains. Every time we had to make the same approach, through the same gap. There was no way to vary our attack. As we dived for the fourteenth time I thought, now that I was free from the fear of humiliation, 'They have only to fix one machine-gun into position.' We lifted our nose again into the safe air – perhaps they didn't even have a gun. The forty minutes of the patrol had seemed interminable, but it had been free from the discomfort of personal thought. The sun was sinking as we turned for home: the geographer's moment had passed: the Black River was no longer black, and the Red River was only gold.

Down we went again, away from the gnarled and fissured forest towards the river, flattening out over the neglected rice-fields, aimed like a bullet at one small sampan on the yellow stream. The cannon gave a single burst of tracer, and the sampan blew apart in a shower of sparks: we didn't even wait to see our victims struggling to survive, but climbed and made for home. I thought again as I had thought when I saw the dead child at Phat Diem, 'I hate war.' There had been something so shocking in our sudden fortuitous choice of a prey – we had just happened to be passing, one burst only was required, there was no one to return our fire, we were gone again, adding our little quota to the world's dead.

I put on my earphones for Captain Trouin to speak to me. He said, 'We will make a little detour. The sunset is wonderful on the *calcaire*. You must not miss it,' he added kindly, like a host who is showing the beauty of his estate, and for a hundred miles we trailed the sunset over the Baie d'Along. The helmeted Martian face looked wistfully out, down the golden groves among the great humps and arches of porous stone, and the wounds of murder ceased to bleed.

5

Captain Trouin insisted that night on being my host in the opium house, though he would not smoke himself. He liked the smell, he said, he liked the sense of quiet at the end of the day, but in his profession relaxation could go no further. There were officers who smoked, but they were Army men – he had to have his sleep. We lay in a small cubicle in a row of cubicles like a dormitory at school, and the Chinese proprietor prepared my pipes. I hadn't smoked since Phuong left me. Across the way a *métisse* with long and lovely legs lay coiled after her smoke reading a glossy woman's paper, and in the cubicle next to her two middle-aged Chinese transacted business, sipping tea, their pipes laid aside.

I said, 'That sampan – this evening – was it doing any harm?'

Trouin said, 'Who knows? In those reaches of the river we have orders to shoot up anything in sight.'

I smoked my first pipe. I tried not to think of all the pipes I had smoked at home. Trouin said, 'Today's affair – that is not the worst for someone like myself. Over the village they could have shot us down. Our risk was as great as theirs. What I detest is napalm bombing. From 3,000 feet, in safety.' He made a hopeless gesture. 'You see the forest catching fire. God knows what you would see from the ground. The poor devils are burnt alive, the flames go over them like water. They are wet through with fire.' He said with anger against a whole world that didn't understand, 'I'm not fighting a colonial war. Do you think I'd do these things for the planters of Terre Rouge? I'd rather be court-martialled. We are fighting all of your wars, but you leave us the guilt.'

'That sampan,' I said.

'Yes, that sampan too.' He watched me as I stretched out for my second pipe. 'I envy you your means of escape.'

'You don't know what I'm escaping from. It's not from the war. That's no concern of mine. I'm not involved.'

'You will all be. One day.'

'Not me.'

'You are still limping.'

'They had the right to shoot at me, but they weren't even doing that. They were knocking down a tower. One should always avoid demolition squads. Even in Piccadilly.'

'One day something will happen. You will take a side.'

'No, I'm going back to England.'

'That photograph you showed me once . . .'

'Oh, I've torn that one up. She left me.'

'I'm sorry.'

'It's the way things happen. One leaves people oneself and then the tide turns. It almost makes me believe in justice.'

'I do. The first time I dropped napalm I thought, this is the village where I was born. That is where M. Dubois, my father's old friend, lives. The baker – I was very fond of the baker when I was a child – is running away down there in the flames I've thrown. The men of Vichy did not bomb their own country. I felt worse than them.'

'But you still go on.'

'Those are moods. They come only with the napalm. The rest of the time I think that I am defending Europe. And you know, those others – they do some monstrous things also. When they were driven out of Hanoi in 1946 they left terrible relics among their own people – people they thought had helped us. There was one girl in the mortuary – they had not only cut off her breasts, they had mutilated her lover and stuffed his . . .'

'That's why I won't be involved.'

'It's not a matter of reason or justice. We all get involved in a moment of emotion and then we cannot get out. War and Love – they have always been compared.' He looked sadly across the dormitory to where the *métisse* sprawled in her great temporary peace. He said, 'I would not have it otherwise. *There* is a girl who was involved by her parents – what is her future when this port falls? France is only half her home . . .'

'Will it fall?'

'You are a journalist. You know better than I do that we can't win. You know the road to Hanoi is cut and mined every night. You know we lose one class of St Cyr every year. We were nearly beaten in '50. De Lattre has given us two years of grace – that's all. But we are professionals: we have to go on fighting till the politicians tell us to stop. Probably they will get together and agree to the same peace that we could have had at the beginning, making nonsense of all these years.' His ugly face which had winked at me before the dive wore a kind of professional brutality like a Christmas mask from which a child's eyes peer through the holes in the paper. 'You would not understand the nonsense, Fowler. You are not one of us.'

'There are other things in one's life which make nonsense of the years.'

He put his hand on my knee with an odd protective gesture as though he were the older man. 'Take her home,' he said. 'That is better than a pipe.'

'How do you know she would come?'

'I have slept with her myself, and Lieutenant Perrin. Five hundred piastres.'

'Expensive.'

'I expect she would go for three hundred, but under the circumstances one does not care to bargain.'

But his advice did not prove sound. A man's body is limited in the acts which it can perform and mine was frozen by memory. What my hands touched that night might be more beautiful than I was used to, but we are not trapped only by beauty. She used the same perfume, and suddenly at the moment of entry the ghost of what I'd lost proved more powerful than the body stretched at my disposal. I moved away and lay on my back and desire drained out of me.

'I am sorry,' I said, and lied, 'I don't know what is the matter with me.'

She said with great sweetness and misunderstanding, 'Don't worry. It often happens that way. It is the opium.'

'Yes,' I said, 'the opium.' And I wished to heaven that it had been.

Chapter 2

1

IT was strange, this first return to Saigon with nobody to welcome me. At the airport I wished there were somewhere else to which I could direct my taxi than the rue Catinat. I thought to myself: 'Is the pain a little less than when I went away?' and tried to persuade myself that it was so. When I reached the landing I saw that the door was open, and I became breathless with an unreasonable hope. I walked very slowly towards the door. Until I reached the door hope would remain alive. I heard a chair creak, and when I came to the door I could see a pair of shoes, but they were not a woman's shoes. I went quickly in, and it was Pyle who lifted his awkward weight from the chair Phuong used to use.

He said, 'Hullo, Thomas.'

'Hullo, Pyle. How did you get in?'

'I met Dominguez. He was bringing your mail. I asked him to let me stay.'

'Has Phuong forgotten something?'

'Oh no, but Joe told me you'd been to the Legation. I thought it would be easier to talk here.'

'What about?'

He gave a lost gesture, like a boy put up to speak at some school function who cannot find the grown-up words. 'You've been away?'

'Yes. And you?'

'Oh, I've been travelling around.'

'Still playing with plastics?'

He grinned unhappily. He said, 'Your letters are over there.'

I could see at a glance there was nothing which could interest me now: there was one from my office in London and several that looked like bills, and one from my bank. I said, 'How's Phuong?'

His face lit up automatically like one of those electric toys which respond to a particular sound. 'Oh, she's fine,' he said, and then clamped his lips together as though he'd gone too far.

'Sit down, Pyle,' I said. 'Excuse me while I look at this. It's from my office.'

I opened it. How inopportunely the unexpected can occur. The editor wrote that he had considered my last letter and that in view of the confused situation in Indo-China, following the death of General de Lattre and the retreat from Hoa Binh, he was in agreement with my suggestion. He had appointed a temporary foreign editor and would like me to stay on in Indo-China for at least another year. 'We shall keep the chair warm for you,' he reassured me with complete incomprehension. He believed I cared about the job, and the paper.

I sat down opposite Pyle and re-read the letter which had come too late. For a moment I had felt elation as on the instant of waking before one remembers.

'Bad news?' Pyle asked.

'No.' I told myself that it wouldn't have made any difference anyway: a reprieve for one year couldn't stand up against a marriage settlement.

'Are you married yet?' I asked.

'No.' He blushed – he had a great facility in blushing. 'As a matter of fact I'm hoping to get special leave. Then we could get married at home – properly.'

'Is it more proper when it happens at home?'

'Well, I thought – it's difficult to say these things to you, you are so darned cynical, Thomas, but it's a mark of respect. My father and mother would be there – she'd kind of enter the family. It's important in view of the past.'

'The past?'

'You know what I mean. I wouldn't want to leave her behind there with any stigma . . .'

'Would you leave her behind?'

'I guess so. My mother's a wonderful woman – she'd take her around, introduce her, you know, kind of fit her in. She'd help her to get a home ready for me.'

I didn't know whether to feel sorry for Phuong or not – she had looked forward so to the skyscrapers and the Statue of Liberty, but she had so little idea of all they would involve,

Professor and Mrs Pyle, the women's lunch clubs; would they teach her Canasta? I thought of her that first night in the Grand Monde, in her white dress, moving so exquisitely on her eighteen-year-old feet, and I thought of her a month ago, bargaining over meat at the butcher's stores in the Boulevard de la Somme. Would she like those bright clean little New England grocery stores where even the celery was wrapped in cellophane? Perhaps she would. I couldn't tell. Strangely I found myself saying as Pyle might have done a month ago, 'Go easy with her, Pyle. Don't force things. She can be hurt like you or me.'

'Of course, of course, Thomas.'

'She looks so small and breakable and unlike our women, but don't think of her as – as an ornament.'

'It's funny, Thomas, how differently things work out. I'd been dreading this talk. I thought you'd be tough.'

'I've had time to think, up in the north. There was a woman there . . . Perhaps I saw what you saw at that whorehouse. It's a good thing she went away with you. I might one day have left her behind with someone like Granger. A piece of tail.'

'And we can remain friends, Thomas?'

'Yes, of course. Only I'd rather not see Phuong. There's quite enough of her around here as it is. I must find another flat – when I've got time.'

He unwound his legs and stood up. 'I'm so glad, Thomas. I can't tell you how glad I am. I've said it before, I know, but I do really wish it hadn't been you.'

'I'm glad it's you, Pyle.' The interview had not been the way I had foreseen: under the superficial angry schemes, at some deeper level, the genuine plan of action must have been formed. All the time that his innocence had angered me, some judge within myself had summed up in his favour, had compared his idealism, his half-baked ideas founded on the works of York Harding, with my cynicism. Oh, I was right about the facts, but wasn't he right too to be young and mistaken, and wasn't he perhaps a better man for a girl to spend her life with?

We shook hands perfunctorily, but some half-formulated fear made me follow him out to the head of the stairs and call after him. Perhaps there is a prophet as well as a judge in those interior courts where our true decisions are made. 'Pyle, don't trust too much in York Harding.'

'York!' He stared up at me from the first landing.

'We are the old colonial peoples, Pyle, but we've learnt a bit of reality, we've learned not to play with matches. This Third Force – it comes out of a book, that's all. General Thé's only a bandit with a few thousand men: he's not a national democracy.'

It was as if he had been staring at me through a letter-box to see who was there and now, letting the flap fall, had shut out the unwelcome intruder. His eyes were out of sight. 'I don't know what you mean, Thomas.'

'Those bicycle bombs. They were a good joke, even though one man did lose a foot. But, Pyle, you can't trust men like Thé. They aren't going to save the East from Communism. We know their kind.'

'We?'

'The old colonialists.'

'I thought you took no sides.'

'I don't, Pyle, but if someone has got to make a mess of things in your outfit, leave it to Joe. Go home with Phuong. Forget the Third Force.'

'Of course I always value your advice, Thomas,' he said formally. 'Well, I'll be seeing you.'

'I suppose so.'

2

The weeks moved on, but somehow I hadn't yet found myself a new flat. It wasn't that I hadn't time. The annual crisis of the war had passed again: the hot wet *crachin* had settled on the north: the French were out of Hoa Binh, the rice-campaign was over in Tonkin and the opium-campaign in Laos. Dominguez could cover easily all that was needed in the south. At last I did drag myself to see one apartment in a so-called modern building (Paris Exhibition 1934?) up at the other end of the rue Catinat beyond the Continental Hotel. It was the Saigon pied-à-terre of a rubber planter who was going home. He wanted to sell it lock, stock and barrel. I have always wondered what the barrels contain: as for the stock, there were a large number of engravings from the Paris Salon between 1880 and 1900. Their highest common factor was a big-bosomed woman with an extraordinary hair-do and gauzy draperies which somehow always exposed the great cleft buttocks and hid the field of battle. In the bathroom the planter had been rather more daring with his reproductions of Rops.

'You like art?' I asked and he smirked back at me like a fellow conspirator. He was fat with a little black moustache and insufficient hair.

'My best pictures are in Paris,' he said.

There was an extraordinary tall ash-tray in the living-room made like a naked woman with a bowl in her hair, and there were china ornaments of naked girls embracing tigers, and one very odd one of a girl stripped to the waist riding a bicycle. In the bedroom facing his enormous bed was a great glazed oil painting of two girls sleeping together. I asked him the price of his apartment without his collection, but he would not agree to separate the two.

'You are not a collector?' he asked.

'Well, no.'

'I have some books also,' he said, 'which I would throw in, though I intended to take these back to France.' He unlocked a glass-fronted bookcase and showed me his library – there were expensive illustrated editions of *Aphrodite* and *Nana*, there was *La Garçonne*, and even several Paul de Kocks. I was tempted to ask him whether he would sell himself with his collection: he went with them: he was period too. He said, 'If you live alone in the tropics a collection is company.'

I thought of Phuong just because of her complete absence. So it always is: when you escape to a desert the silence shouts in your ear.

'I don't think my paper would allow me to buy an art-collection.'

He said, 'It would not, of course, appear on the receipt.'

I was glad Pyle had not seen him: the man might have lent his features to Pyle's imaginary 'old colonialist', who was repulsive enough without him. When I came out it was nearly half past eleven and I went down as far as the Pavillon for a glass of iced beer. The Pavillon was a coffee centre for European and American women and I was confident that I would not see Phuong there. Indeed I knew exactly where she would be at this time of day – she was not a girl to break her habits, and so, coming from the planter's apartment, I had crossed the road to avoid the milk-bar where at this time of day she had her chocolate malt. Two young American girls sat at the next table, neat and clean in the heat, scooping up ice-cream. They each had a bag slung on the left shoulder and the bags were identical, with brass eagle badges. Their legs were identical too, long and slender, and their noses, just a shade tilted, and they were eating their ice-cream with concentration as though they were making an experiment in the college laboratory. I wondered whether they were Pyle's colleagues: they were charming, and I wanted to send them home, too. They finished their ices and one looked at her watch. 'We'd better be going,' she said, 'to be on the safe side.' I wondered idly what appointment they had.

'Warren said we mustn't stay later than eleven twenty-five.'

'It's past that now.'

'It would be exciting to stay. I don't know what it's all about, do you?'

'Not exactly, but Warren said better not.'

'Do you think it's a demonstration?'

'I've seen so many demonstrations,' the other said wearily, like a tourist glutted with churches. She rose and laid on their table the money for the ices. Before going she looked around the café, and the mirrors caught her profile at every freckled angle. There was only myself left and a dowdy middle-aged Frenchwoman who was carefully and uselessly making up her face. Those two hardly needed make-up, the quick dash of lipstick, a comb through the hair. For a moment her glance had rested on me – it was not like a woman's glance, but a man's, very straightforward, speculating on some course of action. Then she turned quickly to her companion. 'We'd better be off.' I watched them idly as they went out side by side into the sun-splintered street. It was impossible to conceive either of them a prey to untidy passion: they did not belong to rumpled sheets and the sweat of sex. Did they take deodorants to bed with them? I found myself for a moment envying them their sterilized world, so different from this world that I inhabited – which suddenly inexplicably broke in pieces. Two of the mirrors on the wall flew at me and collapsed half-way. The dowdy Frenchwoman was on her knees in a wreckage of chairs and tables. Her compact lay open and unhurt in my lap and oddly enough I sat exactly where I had sat before, although my table had joined the wreckage around the Frenchwoman. A curious garden-sound filled the café: the regular drip of a fountain, and looking at the bar I saw rows of smashed bottles which let out their contents in a multi-coloured stream – the red of porto, the orange of cointreau, the green of chartreuse, the cloudy yellow of pastis, across the floor of the café. The Frenchwoman sat up and calmly looked around for her compact. I gave it her and she thanked me formally, sitting on the floor. I realized that I didn't hear her very well. The explosion had been so close that my ear-drums had still to recover from the pressure.

I thought rather petulantly, 'Another joke with plastics: what does Mr Heng expect me to write now?' but when I got into the Place Garnier, I realized by the heavy clouds of smoke that this was no joke. The smoke came from the cars burning in the car-park in front of the national theatre, bits of cars were scattered over the square, and a man without his legs lay twitching at the edge of the ornamental gardens. People were crowding in from the rue Catinat, from the Boulevard Bonnard. The sirens of police-cars, the bells of the ambulances and fire-engines came at one remove to my shocked ear-drums. For one moment I had forgotten that Phuong must have been in the milk-bar on the other side of the square. The smoke lay between. I couldn't see through.

I stepped out into the square and a policeman stopped me. They had formed a cordon round the edge to prevent the crowd increasing, and already the stretchers were beginning to emerge. I implored the policeman in front of me, 'Let me across. I have a friend . . .'

'Stand back,' he said. 'Everybody here has friends.'

He stood on one side to let a priest through, and I tried to follow the priest, but he pulled me back. I said, 'I am the Press,' and searched in vain for the wallet in which I had my card, but I couldn't find it: had I come out that day without it? I said, 'At least tell me what happened to the milk-bar': the smoke was clearing and I tried to see, but the crowd between was too great. He said something I didn't catch.

'What did you say?'

He repeated, 'I don't know. Stand back. You are blocking the stretchers.'

Could I have dropped my wallet in the Pavillon? I turned to go back and there was Pyle. He exclaimed, 'Thomas.'

'Pyle,' I said, 'for Christ's sake, where's your Legation pass? We've got to get across. Phuong's in the milk-bar.'

'No, no,' he said.

'Pyle, she is. She always goes there. At eleven thirty. We've got to find her.'

'She isn't there, Thomas.'

'How do you know? Where's your card?'

'I warned her not to go.'

I turned back to the policeman, meaning to throw him to one side and make a run for it across the square: he might shoot: I didn't care – and then the word 'warn' reached my consciousness. I took Pyle by the arm. 'Warn?' I said. 'What do you mean "warn"?'

'I told her to keep away this morning.'

The pieces fell together in my mind. 'And Warren?' I said. 'Who's Warren? He warned those girls too.'

'I don't understand.'

'There mustn't be any American casualties, must there?'
An ambulance forced its way up the rue Catinat into the square and the policeman who had stopped me moved to one side to let it through. The policeman beside him was engaged in an argument. I pushed Pyle forward and ahead of me into the square before we could be stopped.

We were among a congregation of mourners. The police could prevent others entering the square; they were powerless to clear the square of the survivors and the first-comers. The doctors were too busy to attend to the dead, and so the dead were left to their owners, for one can own the dead as one owns a chair. A woman sat on the ground with what was left of her baby in her lap; with a kind of modesty she had covered it with her straw peasant hat. She was still and silent, and what struck me most in the square was the silence. It was like a church I had once visited during Mass – the only sounds came from those who served, except where here and there the Europeans wept and implored and fell silent again as though shamed by the modesty, patience and propriety of the East. The legless torso at the edge of the garden still twitched, like a chicken which has lost its head. From the man's shirt, he had probably been a trishaw driver.

Pyle said, 'It's awful.' He looked at the wet on his shoes and said in a sick voice, 'What's that?'

'Blood,' I said. 'Haven't you ever seen it before?'

He said, 'I must get them cleaned before I see the Minister.' I don't think he knew what he was saying. He was seeing a real war for the first time: he had punted down into Phat Diem in a kind of schoolboy dream, and anyway in his eyes soldiers didn't count.

I forced him, with my hand on his shoulder, to look around. I said, 'This is the hour when the place is always full of women and children – it's the shopping hour. Why choose that of all hours?'

He said weakly, 'There was to have been a parade.'

'And you hoped to catch a few colonels. But the parade was cancelled yesterday, Pyle.'

'I didn't know.'

'Didn't know!' I pushed him into a patch of blood where a stretcher had lain. 'You ought to be better informed.'

'I was out of town,' he said, looking down at his shoes. 'They should have called it off.'

'And missed the fun?' I asked him. 'Do you expect General Thé to lose his demonstration? This is better than a parade. Women and children are news, and soldiers aren't, in a war. This will hit the world's Press. You've put General Thé on the map all right, Pyle. You've got the Third Force and National Democracy all over your right shoe. Go home to Phuong and tell her about your heroic dead – there are a few dozen less of her people to worry about.'

A small fat priest scampered by, carrying something on a dish under a napkin. Pyle had been silent a long while, and I had nothing more to say. Indeed I had said too much already. He looked white and beaten and ready to faint, and I thought, 'What's the good? he'll always be innocent, you can't blame the innocent, they are always guiltless. All you can do is control them or eliminate them. Innocence is a kind of insanity.'

He said, 'Thé wouldn't have done this. I'm sure he wouldn't. Somebody deceived him. The Communists . . .'

He was impregnably armoured by his good intentions and his ignorance. I left him standing in the square and went on up the rue Catinat to where the hideous pink Cathedral blocked the way. Already people were flocking in: it must have been a comfort to them to be able to pray for the dead to the dead.

Unlike them, I had reason for thankfulness, for wasn't Phuong alive? Hadn't Phuong been 'warned'? But what I remembered was the torso in the square, the baby on its mother's lap. They had not been warned: they had not been sufficiently important. And if the parade had taken place would they not have been there just the same, out of curiosity, to see the soldiers, and hear the speakers, and throw the flowers? A two-hundred-pound bomb does not discriminate. How many dead colonels justify a child's or a trishaw driver's death when you are building a national democratic front? I stopped a motor-trishaw and told the driver to take me to the Quai Mytho.

PART FOUR

Chapter 1

I HAD given Phuong money to take her sister to the cinema so that she would be safely out of the way. I went out to dinner myself with Dominguez and was back in my room waiting when Vigot called sharp on ten. He apologized for not taking a drink – he said he was too tired and a drink might send him to sleep. It had been a very long day.

'Murder and sudden death?'

'No. Petty thefts. And a few suicides. These people love to gamble and when they have lost everything they kill themselves. Perhaps I would not have become a policeman if I had known how much time I would have to spend in mortuaries. I do not like the smell of ammonia. Perhaps after all I will have a beer.'

'I haven't a refrigerator, I'm afraid.'

'Unlike the mortuary. A little English whisky, then?'

I remembered the night I had gone down to the mortuary with him and they had slid out Pyle's body like a tray of ice-cubes.

'So you are not going home?' he asked.

'You've been checking up?'

'Yes.'

I held the whisky out to him, so that he could see how calm my nerves were. 'Vigot, I wish you'd tell me why you think I was concerned in Pyle's death. Is it a question of motive? That I wanted Phuong back? Or do you imagine it was revenge for losing her?'

'No. I'm not so stupid. One doesn't take one's enemy's book as a souvenir. There it is on your shelf. *The Rôle of the West*. Who is this York Harding?'

'He's the man you are looking for, Vigot. He killed Pyle – at long range.'

'I don't understand.'

'He's a superior sort of journalist – they call them diplomatic correspondents. He gets hold of an idea and then alters

167

every situation to fit the idea. Pyle came out here full of York Harding's idea. Harding had been here once for a week on his way from Bangkok to Tokyo. Pyle made the mistake of putting his idea into practice. Harding wrote about a Third Force. Pyle formed one – a shoddy little bandit with two thousand men and a couple of tame tigers. He got mixed up.'

'You never do, do you?'

'I've tried not to be.'

'But you failed, Fowler.' For some reason I thought of Captain Trouin and that night which seemed to have happened years ago in the Haiphong opium house. What was it he had said? something about all of us getting involved sooner or later in a moment of emotion. I said, 'You would have made a good priest, Vigot. What is it about you that would make it so easy to confess – if there were anything to confess?'

'I have never wanted any confessions.'

'But you've received them?'

'From time to time.'

'Is it because like a priest it's your job not to be shocked, but to be sympathetic? "M. Flic, I must tell you exactly why I battered in the old lady's skull." "Yes, Gustave, take your time and tell me why it was."'

'You have a whimsical imagination. Aren't you drinking, Fowler?'

'Surely it's unwise for a criminal to drink with a police officer?'

'I have never said you were a criminal.'

'But suppose the drink unlocked even in me the desire to confess? There are no secrets of the confessional in your profession.'

'Secrecy is seldom important to a man who confesses: even when it's to a priest. He has other motives.'

'To cleanse himself?'

'Not always. Sometimes he only wants to see himself clearly as he is. Sometimes he is just weary of deception. You are not a criminal, Fowler, but I would like to know why you lied to me. You saw Pyle the night he died.'

'What gives you that idea?'

'I don't for a moment think you killed him. You would hardly have used a rusty bayonet.'

'Rusty?'

'Those are the kind of details we get from an autopsy. I told you, though, that was not the cause of death. Dakow mud.' He held out his glass for another whisky. 'Let me see now. You had a drink at the Continental at six ten?'

'Yes.'

'And at six forty-five you were talking to another journalist at the door of the Majestic?'

'Yes, Wilkins. I told you all this, Vigot, before. That night.'

'Yes. I've checked up since then. It's wonderful how you carry such petty details in your head.'

'I'm a reporter, Vigot.'

'Perhaps the times are not quite accurate, but nobody could blame you, could they, if you were a quarter of an hour out here and ten minutes out there. You had no reason to think the times important. Indeed how suspicious it would be if you had been completely accurate.'

'Haven't I been?'

'Not quite. It was at five to seven that you talked to Wilkins.'

'Another ten minutes.'

'Of course. As I said. And it had only just struck six when you arrived at the Continental.'

'My watch is always a little fast,' I said. 'What time do you make it now?'

'Ten eight.'

'Ten eighteen by mine. You see.'

He didn't bother to look. He said, 'Then the time you said you talked to Wilkins was twenty-five minutes out – by your watch. That's quite a mistake, isn't it?'

'Perhaps I readjusted the time in my mind. Perhaps I'd corrected my watch that day. I sometimes do.'

'What interests me,' Vigot said, '(could I have a little more soda? – you have made this rather strong) is that you are not at all angry with me. It is not very nice to be questioned as I am questioning you.'

169

'I find it interesting, like a detective-story. And, after all, you know I didn't kill Pyle – you've said so.'

Vigot said, 'I know you were not present at his murder.'

'I don't know what you hope to prove by showing that I was ten minutes out here and five there.'

'It gives a little space,' Vigot said, 'a little gap in time.'

'Space for what?'

'For Pyle to come and see you.'

'Why do you want so much to prove that?'

'Because of the dog,' Vigot said.

'And the mud between its toes?'

'It wasn't mud. It was cement. You see, somewhere that night, when it was following Pyle, it stepped into wet cement. I remembered that on the ground-floor of the apartment there are builders at work – they are still at work. I passed them tonight as I came in. They work long hours in this country.'

'I wonder how many houses have builders in them – and wet cement. Did any of them remember the dog?'

'Of course I asked them that. But if they had they would not have told me. I am the police.' He stopped talking and leant back in his chair, staring at his glass. I had a sense that some analogy had struck him and he was miles away in thought. A fly crawled over the back of his hand and he did not brush it away – any more than Dominguez would have done. I had the feeling of some force immobile and profound. For all I knew, he might have been praying.

I rose and went through the curtains into the bedroom. There was nothing I wanted there, except to get away for a moment from that silence sitting in a chair. Phuong's picture-books were back on the shelf. She had stuck a telegram for me up among the cosmetics – some message or other from the London office. I wasn't in the mood to open it. Everything was as it had been before Pyle came. Rooms don't change, ornaments stand where you place them: only the heart decays.

I returned to the sitting-room and Vigot put the glass to his lips. I said, 'I've got nothing to tell you. Nothing at all.'

'Then I'll be going,' he said. 'I don't suppose I'll trouble you again.'

At the door he turned as though he were unwilling to

abandon hope – his hope or mine. 'That was a strange picture for you to go and see that night. I wouldn't have thought you cared for costume drama. What was it? *Robin Hood?*'

'*Scaramouche*, I think. I had to kill time. And I needed distraction.'

'Distraction?'

'We all have our private worries, Vigot,' I carefully explained.

When Vigot was gone there was still an hour to wait for Phuong and living company. It was strange how disturbed I had been by Vigot's visit. It was as though a poet had brought me his work to criticize and through some careless action I had destroyed it. I was a man without a vocation – one cannot seriously consider journalism as a vocation, but I could recognize a vocation in another. Now that Vigot was gone to close his uncompleted file, I wished I had the courage to call him back and say, 'You are right. I did see Pyle the night he died.'

Chapter 2

1

ON the way to the Quai Mytho I passed several ambulances driving out of Cholon heading for the Place Garnier. One could almost reckon the pace of rumour from the expression of the faces in the street, which at first turned on someone like myself coming from the direction of the Place with looks of expectancy and speculation. By the time I entered Cholon I had outstripped the news: life was busy, normal, uninterrupted: nobody knew.

I found Mr Chou's godown and mounted to Mr Chou's house. Nothing had changed since my last visit. The cat and the dog moved from floor to cardboard box to suitcase, like a couple of chess knights who cannot get to grips. The baby crawled on the floor, and the two old men were still playing mah jongg. Only the young people were absent. As soon as I appeared in the doorway one of the women began to pour out tea. The old lady sat on the bed and looked at her feet.

'Monsieur Heng,' I asked. I shook my head at the tea: I wasn't in the mood to begin another long course of that trivial bitter brew. 'Il faut absolument que je voie Monsieur Heng.' It seemed impossible to convey to them the urgency of my request, but perhaps the very abruptness of my refusal of tea caused some disquiet. Or perhaps like Pyle I had blood on my shoes. Anyway after a short delay one of the women led me out and down the stairs, along two bustling bannered streets and left me before what they would have called I suppose in Pyle's country a 'funeral parlour', full of stone jars in which the resurrected bones of the Chinese dead are eventually placed. 'Monsieur Heng,' I said to an old Chinese in the doorway, 'Monsieur Heng.' It seemed a suitable halting place on a day which had begun with the planter's erotic collection and continued with the murdered bodies in the square. Somebody called from an inner room and the Chinese stepped aside and let me in.

Mr Heng himself came cordially forward and ushered me into a little inner room lined with the black carved uncomfortable chairs you find in every Chinese ante-room, unused, unwelcoming. But I had the sense that on this occasion the chairs had been employed, for there were five little tea-cups on the table, and two were not empty. 'I have interrupted a meeting,' I said.

'A matter of business,' Mr Heng said evasively, 'of no importance. I am always glad to see you, Mr Fowler.'

'I've come from the Place Garnier,' I said.

'I thought that was it.'

'You've heard . . .'

'Someone telephoned to me. It was thought best that I keep away from Mr Chou's for a while. The police will be very active today.'

'But you had nothing to do with it.'

'It is the business of the police to find a culprit.'

'It was Pyle again,' I said.

'Yes.'

'It was a terrible thing to do.'

'General Thé is not a very controlled character.'

'And bombs aren't for boys from Boston. Who is Pyle's chief, Heng?'

'I have the impression that Mr Pyle is very much his own master.'

'What is he? O.S.S.?'

'The initial letters are not very important. I think now they are different.'

'What can I do, Heng? He's got to be stopped.'

'You can publish the truth. Or perhaps you cannot?'

'My paper's not interested in General Thé. They are only interested in your people, Heng.'

'You really want Mr Pyle stopped, Mr Fowler?'

'If you'd seen him, Heng. He stood there and said it was all a sad mistake, there should have been a parade. He said he'd have to get his shoes cleaned before he saw the Minister.'

'Of course, you could tell what you know to the police.'

'They aren't interested in Thé either. And do you think they would dare to touch an American? He has diplomatic privileges. He's a graduate of Harvard. The Minister's very fond of Pyle. Heng, there was a woman there whose baby – she kept it covered under her straw hat. I can't get it out of my head. And there was another in Phat Diem.'

'You must try to be calm, Mr Fowler.'

'What'll he do next, Heng?'

'Would you be prepared to help us, Mr Fowler?'

'He comes blundering in and people have to die for his mistakes. I wish your people had got him on the river from Nam Dinh. It would have made a lot of difference to a lot of lives.'

'I agree with you, Mr Fowler. He has to be restrained. I have a suggestion to make.' Somebody coughed delicately behind the door, then noisily spat. He said, 'If you would invite him to dinner tonight at the Vieux Moulin. Between eight thirty and nine thirty.'

'What good . . . ?'

'We would talk to him on the way,' Heng said.

'He may be engaged'

'Perhaps it would be better if you asked him to call on you – at six thirty. He will be free then: he will certainly come. If he is able to have dinner with you, take a book to your window as though you want to catch the light.'

'Why the Vieux Moulin?'

'It is by the bridge to Dakow – I think we shall be able to find a spot and talk undisturbed.'

'What will you do?'

'You do not want to know that, Mr Fowler. But I promise you we will act as gently as the situation allows.'

The unseen friends of Heng shifted like rats behind the wall. 'Will you do this for us, Mr Fowler?'

'I don't know,' I said, 'I don't know.'

'Sooner or later,' Heng said, and I was reminded of Captain Trouin speaking in the opium house, 'one has to take sides. If one is to remain human.'

2

I left a note at the Legation asking Pyle to come and then I went up the street to the Continental for a drink. The wreckage was all cleared away; the fire-brigade had hosed the square. I had no idea then how the time and the place would become important. I even thought of sitting there throughout the evening and breaking my appointment. Then I thought that perhaps I could frighten Pyle into inactivity by warning him of his danger – whatever his danger was, and so I finished my beer and went home, and when I reached home I began to hope that Pyle would not come. I tried to read, but there was nothing on my shelves to hold the attention. Perhaps I should have smoked, but there was no one to prepare my pipe. I listened unwillingly for footsteps and at last they came. Somebody knocked. I opened the door, but it was only Dominguez.

I said, 'What do you want, Dominguez?'

He looked at me with an air of surprise. 'Want?' He looked at his watch. 'This is the time I always come. Have you any cables?'

'I'm sorry – I'd forgotten. No.'

'But a follow-up on the bomb? Don't you want something filed?'

'Oh, work one out for me, Dominguez. I don't know how it is – being there on the spot, perhaps I got a bit shocked. I can't think of the thing in terms of a cable.' I hit out at a mosquito which came droning at my ear and saw Dominguez wince instinctively at my blow. 'It's all right, Dominguez, I missed it.' He grinned miserably. He could not justify this reluctance to take life: after all he was a Christian – one of those who had learnt from Nero how to make human bodies into candles.

'Is there anything I can do for you?' he asked. He didn't drink, he didn't eat meat, he didn't kill – I envied him the gentleness of his mind.

'No, Dominguez. Just leave me alone tonight.' I watched him from the window, going away across the rue Catinat. A trishaw driver had parked beside the pavement opposite my window; Dominguez tried to engage him, but the man shook his head. Presumably he was waiting for a client in one of the shops, for this was not a parking place for trishaws. When I looked at my watch it was strange to see that I had been waiting for little more than ten minutes, and, when Pyle knocked, I hadn't even heard his step.

'Come in.' But as usual it was the dog that came in first.

'I was glad to get your note, Thomas. This morning I thought you were mad at me.'

'Perhaps I was. It wasn't a pretty sight.'

'You know so much now, it won't hurt to tell you a bit more. I saw Thé this afternoon.'

'Saw him? Is he in Saigon? I suppose he came to see how his bomb worked.'

'That's in confidence, Thomas. I dealt with him very severely.' He spoke like the captain of a school-team who has found one of his boys breaking his training. All the same I asked him with a certain hope, 'Have you thrown him over?'

'I told him that if he made another uncontrolled demonstration we would have no more to do with him.'

'But haven't you finished with him already, Pyle?' I pushed impatiently at his dog which was nosing around my ankles.

'I can't. (Sit down, Duke.) In the long run he's the only hope we have. If he came to power with our help, we could rely on him . . .'

'How many people have to die before you realize . . . ?' But I could tell that it was a hopeless argument.

'Realize what, Thomas?'

'That there's no such thing as gratitude in politics.'

'At least they won't hate us like they hate the French.'

'Are you sure? Sometimes we have a kind of love for our enemies and sometimes we feel hate for our friends.'

'You talk like a European, Thomas. These people aren't complicated.'

'Is that what you've learned in a few months? You'll be calling them childlike next.'

'Well – in a way.'

'Find me an uncomplicated child, Pyle. When we are young we are a jungle of complications. We simplify as we get older.' But what good was it to talk to him? There was an unreality in both our arguments. I was becoming a leader-writer before my time. I got up and went to the bookshelf.

176

'What are you looking for, Thomas?'

'Oh, just a passage I used to be fond of. Can you have dinner with me, Pyle?'

'I'd love to, Thomas. I'm so glad you aren't mad any longer. I know you disagree with me, but we can disagree, can't we, and be friends?'

'I don't know. I don't think so.'

'After all, Phuong was much more important than this.'

'Do you really believe that, Pyle?'

'Why, she's the most important thing there is. To me. And to you, Thomas.'

'Not to me any longer.'

'It was a terrible shock today, Thomas, but in a week, you'll see, we'll have forgotten it. We are looking after the relatives too.'

'We?'

'We've wired to Washington. We'll get permission to use some of our funds.'

I interrupted him. 'The Vieux Moulin? Between nine and nine thirty?'

'Where you like, Thomas.' I went to the window. The sun had sunk below the roofs. The trishaw driver still waited for his fare. I looked down at him and he raised his face to me.

'Are you waiting for someone, Thomas?'

'No. There was just a piece I was looking for.' To cover my action I read, holding the book up to the last light:

> '*I drive through the streets and I care not a damn,*
> *The people they stare, and they ask who I am;*
> *And if I should chance to run over a cad,*
> *I can pay for the damage if ever so bad.*
> *So pleasant it is to have money, heigh ho!*
> *So pleasant it is to have money.*'

'That's a funny kind of poem,' Pyle said with a note of disapproval.

'He was an adult poet in the nineteenth century. There weren't so many of them.' I looked down into the street again. The trishaw driver had moved away.

'Have you run out of drink?' Pyle asked.

'No, but I thought you didn't . . .'

'Perhaps I'm beginning to loosen up,' Pyle said. 'Your influence. I guess you're good for me, Thomas.'

I got the bottle and glasses – I forgot one of them the first journey and then I had to go back for water. Everything that I did that evening took a long time. He said, 'You know, I've got a wonderful family, but maybe they were a little on the strict side. We have one of those old houses in Chestnut Street, as you go up the hill on the right-hand side. My mother collects glass, and my father – when he's not eroding his old cliffs – picks up all the Darwin manuscripts and association-copies he can. You see, they live in the past. Maybe that's why York made such an impression on me. He seemed kind of open to modern conditions. My father's an isolationist.'

'Perhaps I would like your father,' I said. 'I'm an isolationist too.'

For a quiet man Pyle that night was in a talking mood. I didn't hear all that he said, for my mind was elsewhere. I tried to persuade myself that Mr Heng had other means at his disposal but the crude and obvious one. But in a war like this, I knew, there is no time to hesitate: one uses the weapon to hand – the French the napalm bomb, Mr Heng the bullet or the knife. I told myself too late that I wasn't made to be a judge – I would let Pyle talk awhile and then I would warn him. He could spend the night at my house. They would hardly break in there. I think he was speaking of the old nurse he had had – 'She really meant more to me than my mother, and the blueberry pies she used to make!' when I interrupted him. 'Do you carry a gun now – since that night?'

'No. We have orders in the Legation . . .'

'But you're on special duties?'

'It wouldn't do any good – if they wanted to get me, they always could. Anyway I'm as blind as a coot. At college they called me Bat – because I could see in the dark as well as they could. Once when we were fooling around . . .' He was off again. I returned to the window.

A trishaw driver waited opposite. I wasn't sure – they looked so much alike, but I thought he was a different one. Perhaps he really had a client. It occurred to me that Pyle would be safest at the Legation. They must have laid their plans, since my signal, for later in the evening: something that involved the Dakow bridge. I couldn't understand why or how: surely he would not be so foolish as to drive through Dakow after sunset and our side of the bridge was always guarded by armed police.

'I'm doing all the talking,' Pyle said. 'I don't know how it is, but somehow this evening . . .'

'Go on,' I said, 'I'm in a quiet mood, that's all. Perhaps we'd better cancel that dinner.'

'No, don't do that. I've felt cut off from you, since . . . well . . .'

'Since you saved my life,' I said and couldn't disguise the bitterness of my self-inflicted wound.

'No, I didn't mean that. All the same how we talked, didn't we, that night? As if it was going to be our last. I learned a lot about you, Thomas. I don't agree with you, mind, but for you maybe it's right – not being involved. You kept it up all right, even after your leg was smashed you stayed neutral.'

'There's always a point of change,' I said. 'Some moment of emotion . . .'

'You haven't reached it yet. I doubt if you ever will. And I'm not likely to change either – except with death,' he added merrily.

'Not even with this morning? Mightn't that change a man's views?'

'They were only war casualties,' he said. 'It was a pity, but you can't always hit your target. Anyway they died in the right cause.'

'Would you have said the same if it had been your old nurse with her blueberry pie?'

He ignored my facile point. 'In a way you could say they died for democracy,' he said.

'I wouldn't know how to translate that into Vietnamese.' I was suddenly very tired. I wanted him to go away quickly and die. Then I could start life again – at the point before he came in.

'You'll never take me seriously, will you, Thomas?' he

complained, with that schoolboy gaiety which he seemed to have kept up his sleeve for this night of all nights. 'I tell you what – Phuong's at the cinema – what about you and me spending the whole evening together? I've nothing to do now.' It was as though someone from outside were directing him how to choose his words in order to rob me of any possible excuse. He went on. 'Why don't we go to the Chalet? I haven't been there since that night. The food is just as good as the Vieux Moulin, and there's music.'

I said, 'I'd rather not remember that night.'

'I'm sorry. I'm a dumb fool sometimes, Thomas. What about a Chinese dinner in Cholon?'

'To get a good one you have to order in advance. Are you scared of the Vieux Moulin, Pyle? It's well wired and there are always police on the bridge. And you wouldn't be such a fool, would you, as to drive through Dakow?'

'It wasn't that. I just thought it would be fun tonight to make a long evening of it.'

He made a movement and upset his glass, which smashed upon the floor. 'Good luck,' he said mechanically. 'I'm sorry, Thomas.' I began to pick up the pieces and pack them into the ash-tray. 'What about it, Thomas?' The smashed glass reminded me of the bottles in the Pavillon bar dripping their contents. 'I warned Phuong I might be out with you.' How badly chosen was the word 'warn'. I picked up the last piece of glass. 'I have got an engagement at the Majestic,' I said, 'and I can't manage before nine.'

'Well, I guess I'll have to go back to the office. Only I'm always afraid of getting caught.'

There was no harm in giving him that one chance. 'Don't mind being late,' I said. 'If you do get caught, look in here later. I'll come back at ten, if you can't make dinner, and wait for you.'

'I'll let you know . . .'

'Don't bother. Just come to the Vieux Moulin – or meet me here.' I handed back the decision to that Somebody in whom I didn't believe: You can intervene if You want to: a telegram on his desk: a message from the Minister. You cannot exist unless you have the power to alter the future. 'Go

180

away now, Pyle. There are things I have to do.' I felt a strange exhaustion, hearing him go away and the pad of his dog's paws.

3

There were no trishaw drivers nearer than the rue d'Ormay when I went out. I walked down to the Majestic and stood awhile watching the unloading of the American bombers. The sun had gone and they worked by the light of arc-lamps. I had no idea of creating an alibi, but I told Pyle I was going to the Majestic and I felt an unreasoning dislike of telling more lies than were needed.

'Evening, Fowler.' It was Wilkins.

'Evening.'

'How's the leg?'

'No trouble now.'

'Got a good story filed?'

'I left it to Dominguez.'

'Oh, they told me you were there.'

'Yes, I was. But space is tight these days. They won't want much.'

'The spice has gone out of the dish, hasn't it?' Wilkins said. 'We ought to have lived in the days of Russell and the old *Times*. Dispatches by balloon. One had time to do some fancy writing then. Why, he'd even have made a column out of *this*. The luxury hotel, the bombers, night falling. Night never falls nowadays, does it, at so many piastres a word.' From far up in the sky you could faintly hear the noise of laughter: somebody broke a glass as Pyle had done. The sound fell on us like icicles. '"The lamps shone o'er fair women and brave men,"' Wilkins malevolently quoted. 'Doing anything tonight, Fowler? Care for a spot of dinner?'

'I'm dining as it is. At the Vieux Moulin.'

'I wish you joy. Granger will be there. They ought to advertise special Granger nights. For those who like background noise.'

I said good night to him and went into the cinema next door – Errol Flynn, or it may have been Tyrone Power (I don't know how to distinguish them in tights), swung on ropes and leapt from balconies and rode bareback into technicolour dawns. He rescued a girl and killed ·his enemy and led a charmed life. It was what they call a film for boys, but the sight of Oedipus emerging with his bleeding eyeballs from the palace at Thebes would surely give a better training for life today. No life is charmed. Luck had been with Pyle at Phat Diem and on the road from Tanyin, but luck doesn't last, and they had two hours to see that no charm worked. A French soldier sat beside me with his hand in a girl's lap, and I envied the simplicity of his happiness or his misery, whichever it might be. I left before the film was over and took a trishaw to the Vieux Moulin.

The restaurant was wired in against grenades and two armed policemen were on duty at the end of the bridge. The *patron*, who had grown fat on his own rich Burgundian cooking, let me through the wire himself. The place smelt of capons and melting butter in the heavy evening heat.

'Are you joining the party of M. Granjair?' he asked me.

'No.'

'A table for one?' It was then for the first time that I thought of the future and the questions I might have to answer. 'For one,' I said, and it was almost as though I had said aloud that Pyle was dead.

There was only one room and Granger's party occupied a large table at the back; the *patron* gave me a small one closest to the wire. There were no window-panes, for fear of splintered glass. I recognized a few of the people Granger was entertaining, and I bowed to them before I sat down: Granger himself looked away. I hadn't seen him for months – only once since the night Pyle fell in love. Perhaps some offensive remark I had made that evening had penetrated the alcoholic fog, for he sat scowling at the head of the table while Madame Desprez, the wife of a public-relations officer, and Captain Duparc of the Press Liaison Service nodded and becked. There was a big man whom I think was an *hôtelier* from Pnom Penh and a French girl I'd never seen before and two or three other faces that I had only observed in bars. It seemed for once to be a quiet party.

I ordered a pastis because I wanted to give Pyle time to

come – plans go awry and so long as I did not begin to eat my dinner it was as though I still had time to hope. And then I wondered what I hoped for. Good luck to the O.S.S. or whatever his gang were called? Long life to plastic bombs and General Thé? Or did I – I of all people – hope for some kind of miracle: a method of discussion arranged by Mr Heng which wasn't simply death? How much easier it would have been if we had both been killed on the road from Tanyin. I sat for twenty minutes over my pastis and then I ordered dinner. It would soon be half past nine: he wouldn't come now.

Against my will I listened: for what? a scream? a shot? some movement by the police outside? but in any case I would probably hear nothing, for Granger's party was warming up. The *hôtelier,* who had a pleasant untrained voice, began to sing and as a new champagne cork popped others joined in, but not Granger. He sat there with raw eyes glaring across the room at me. I wondered if there would be a fight: I was no match for Granger.

They were singing a sentimental song, and as I sat hungerless over my apology for a *Chapon duc Charles* I thought, for almost the first time since I had known that she was safe, of Phuong. I remembered how Pyle, sitting on the floor waiting for the Viets, had said, 'She seems fresh like a flower,' and I had flippantly replied, 'Poor flower.' She would never see New England now or learn the secrets of Canasta. Perhaps she would never know security: what right had I to value her less than the dead bodies in the square? Suffering is not increased by numbers: one body can contain all the suffering the world can feel. I had judged like a journalist in terms of quantity and I had betrayed my own principles; I had become as *engagé* as Pyle, and it seemed to me that no decision would ever be simple again. I looked at my watch and it was nearly a quarter to ten. Perhaps, after all, he had been caught; perhaps that 'someone' in whom he believed had acted on his behalf and he sat now in his Legation room fretting at a telegram to decode, and soon he would come stamping up the stairs to my room in the rue Catinat. I thought, 'If he does I shall tell him everything.'

Granger suddenly got up from his table and came at me. He didn't even see the chair in his way and he stumbled and laid his hand on the edge of my table. 'Fowler,' he said, 'come outside.' I laid enough notes down and followed him. I was in no mood to fight with him, but at that moment I would not have minded if he had beaten me unconscious. We have so few ways in which to assuage the sense of guilt.

He leant on the parapet of the bridge and the two policemen watched him from a distance. He said, 'I've got to talk to you, Fowler.'

I came within striking distance and waited. He didn't move. He was like an emblematic statue of all I thought I hated in America – as ill-designed as the Statue of Liberty and as meaningless. He said without moving, 'You think I'm pissed. You're wrong.'

'What's up, Granger?'

'I got to talk to you, Fowler. I don't want to sit there with those Frogs tonight. I don't like you, Fowler, but you talk English. A kind of English.' He leant there, bulky and shapeless in the half-light, an unexplored continent.

'What do you want, Granger?'

'I don't like Limies,' Granger said. 'I don't know why Pyle stomachs you. Maybe it's because he's Boston. I'm Pittsburgh and proud of it.'

'Why not?'

'There you are again.' He made a feeble attempt to mock my accent. 'You all talk like poufs. You're so damned superior. You think you know everything.'

'Good night, Granger. I've got an appointment.'

'Don't go, Fowler. Haven't you got a heart? I can't talk to those Froggies.'

'You're drunk.'

'I've had two glasses of champagne, that's all, and wouldn't you be drunk in my place? I've got to go north.'

'What's wrong in that?'

'Oh, I didn't tell you, did I? I keep on thinking everyone knows. I got a cable this morning from my wife.'

'Yes?'

'My son's got polio. He's bad.'

184

'I'm sorry.'

'You needn't be. It's not your kid.'

'Can't you fly home?'

'I can't. They want a story about some damned mopping-up operations near Hanoi and Connolly's sick.' (Connolly was his assistant.)

'I'm sorry, Granger. I wish I could help.'

'It's his birthday tonight. He's eight at half past ten our time. That's why I laid on a party with champagne before I knew. I had to tell someone, Fowler, and I can't tell these Froggies.'

'They can do a lot for polio nowadays.'

'I don't mind if he's crippled, Fowler. Not if he lives. Me, I'd be no good crippled, but he's got brains. Do you know what I've been doing in there while that bastard was singing? I was praying. I thought maybe if God wanted a life he could take mine.'

'Do you believe in a God, then?'

'I wish I did,' Granger said. He passed his whole hand across his face as though his head ached, but the motion was meant to disguise the fact that he was wiping tears away.

'I'd get drunk if I were you,' I said.

'Oh, no, I've got to stay sober. I don't want to think afterwards I was stinking drunk the night my boy died. My wife can't drink, can she?'

'Can't you tell your paper . . . ?'

'Connolly's not really sick. He's off after a bit of tail in Singapore. I've got to cover for him. He'd be sacked if they knew.' He gathered his shapeless body together. 'Sorry I kept you, Fowler. I just had to tell someone. Got to go in now and start the toasts. Funny it happened to be you, and you hate my guts.'

'I'd do your story for you. I could pretend it was Connolly.'

'You wouldn't get the accent right.'

'I don't dislike you, Granger. I've been blind to a lot of things . . .'

'Oh, you and me, we're cat and dog. But thanks for the sympathy.'

Was I so different from Pyle, I wondered? Must I too have

185

my foot thrust in the mess of life before I saw the pain? Granger went inside and I could hear the voices rising to greet him. I found a trishaw and was pedalled home. There was nobody there, and I sat and waited till midnight. Then I went down into the street without hope and found Phuong there.

Chapter 3

'HAS Monsieur Vigot been to see you?' Phuong asked.

'Yes. He left a quarter of an hour ago. Was the film good?' She had already laid out the tray in the bedroom and now she was lighting the lamp.

'It was very sad,' she said, 'but the colours were lovely. What did Monsieur Vigot want?'

'He wanted to ask me some questions.'

'What about?'

'This and that. I don't think he will bother me again.'

'I like films with happy endings best,' Phuong said. 'Are you ready to smoke?'

'Yes.' I lay down on the bed and Phuong set to work with her needle. She said, 'They cut off the girl's head.'

'What a strange thing to do.'

'It was in the French Revolution.'

'Oh. Historical. I see.'

'It was very sad all the same.'

'I can't worry much about people in history.'

'And her lover – he went back to his garret – and he was miserable and he wrote a song – you see, he was a poet, and soon all the people who had cut off the head of his girl were singing his song. It was the Marseillaise.'

'It doesn't sound very historical,' I said.

'He stood there at the edge of the crowd while they were singing, and he looked very bitter and when he smiled you knew he was even more bitter and that he was thinking of her. I cried a lot and so did my sister.'

'Your sister? I can't believe it.'

'She is very sensitive. That horrid man Granger was there. He was drunk and he kept on laughing. But it was not funny at all. It was sad.'

'I don't blame him,' I said. 'He has something to celebrate. His son's out of danger. I heard today at the Continental. I like happy endings too.'

After I had smoked two pipes I lay back with my neck on the leather pillow and rested my hand in Phuong's lap. 'Are you happy?'

'Of course,' she said carelessly. I hadn't deserved a more considered answer.

'It's like it used to be,' I lied, 'a year ago.'

'Yes.'

'You haven't bought a scarf for a long time. Why don't you go shopping tomorrow?'

'It is a feast day.'

'Oh yes, of course. I forgot.'

'You have not opened your telegram,' Phuong said.

'No, I'd forgotten that too. I don't want to think about work tonight. And it's too late to file anything now. Tell me more about the film.'

'Well, her lover tried to rescue her from prison. He smuggled in boy's clothes and a man's cap like the one the gaoler wore, but just as she was passing the gate all her hair fell down and they called out "*Une aristocrate, une aristocrate*". I think that was a mistake in the story. They ought to have let her escape. Then they would both have made a lot of money with his song and they would have gone abroad to America – or England,' she added with what she thought was cunning.

'I'd better read the telegram,' I said. 'I hope to God I don't have to go north tomorrow. I want to be quiet with you.'

She loosed the envelope from among the pots of cream and gave it to me. I opened it and read: 'Have thought over your letter again stop am acting irrationally as you hoped stop have told my lawyer start divorce proceedings grounds desertion stop God bless you affectionately Helen.'

'Do you have to go?'

'No,' I said, 'I don't have to go. I'll read it to you. Here's your happy ending.'

She jumped from the bed. 'But it is wonderful. I must go and tell my sister. She will be so pleased. I will say to her, "Do you know who I am? I am the second Mrs Fowlair."'

Opposite me in the bookcase *The Rôle of the West* stood out like a cabinet portrait – of a young man with a crew-cut and a black dog at his heels. He could harm no one any more. I said to Phuong, 'Do you miss him much?'

'Who?'

'Pyle.' Strange how even now, even to her, it was impossible to use his first name.

'Can I go, please? My sister will be so excited.'

'You spoke his name once in your sleep.'

'I never remember my dreams.'

'There was so much you could have done together. He was young.'

'You are not old.'

'The skyscrapers. The Empire State Building.'

She said with a small hesitation, 'I want to see the Cheddar Gorge.'

'It isn't the Grand Canyon.' I pulled her down on to the bed. 'I'm sorry, Phuong.'

'What are you sorry for? It is a wonderful telegram. My sister . . .'

'Yes, go and tell your sister. Kiss me first.' Her excited mouth skated over my face, and she was gone.

I thought of the first day and Pyle sitting beside me at the Continental, with his eye on the soda-fountain across the way. Everything had gone right with me since he had died, but how I wished there existed someone to whom I could say that I was sorry.

March 1952 – *June* 1955

MORE ABOUT PENGUINS
AND PELICANS

Penguinews, which appears every month, contains details of all the new books issued by Penguins as they are published. From time to time it is supplemented by *Penguins in Print*, which is a complete list of all titles available. (There are some five thousand of these.)

A specimen copy of *Penguinews* will be sent to you free on request. For a year's issues (including the complete lists) please send 50p if you live in the British Isles, or 75p if you live elsewhere. Just write to Dept EP, Penguin Books Ltd, Harmondsworth, Middlesex, enclosing a cheque or postal order, and your name will be added to the mailing list.

In the U.S.A.: For a complete list of books available from Penguin in the United States write to Dept CS, Penguin Books Inc., 7110 Ambassador Road, Baltimore, Maryland 21207.

In Canada: For a complete list of books available from Penguin in Canada write to Penguin Books Canada Ltd, 41 Steelcase Road West, Markham, Ontario.